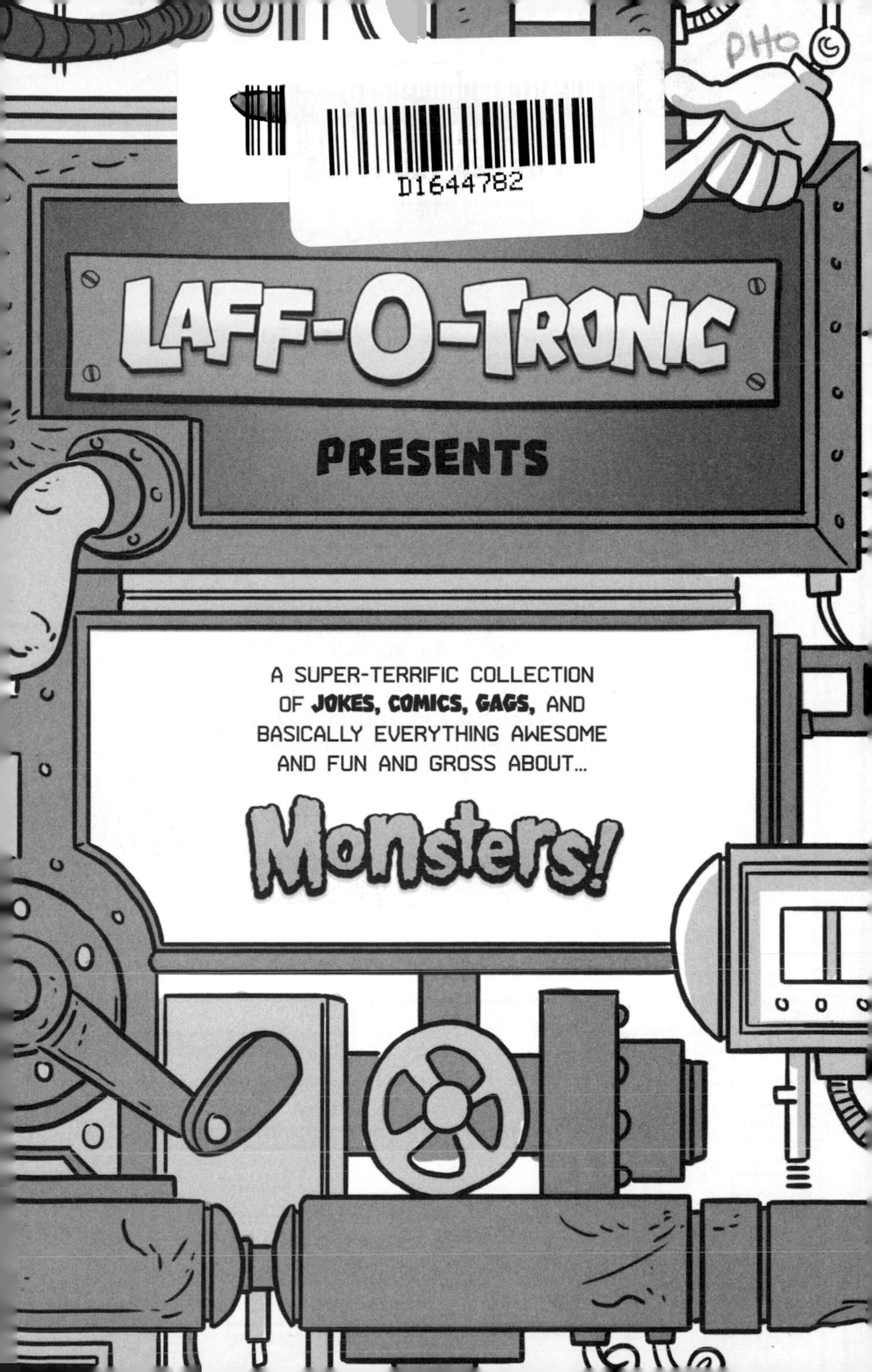
LAFF-O-TRONIC
PRESENTS
A SUPER-TERRIFIC COLLECTION OF JOKES, COMICS, GAGS, AND BASICALLY EVERYTHING AWESOME AND FUN AND GROSS ABOUT...
Monsters!

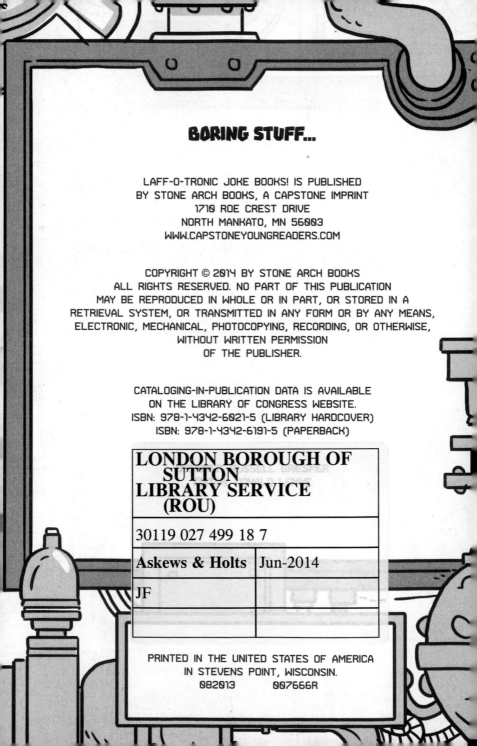

BORING STUFF...

LAFF-O-TRONIC JOKE BOOKS! IS PUBLISHED
BY STONE ARCH BOOKS, A CAPSTONE IMPRINT
1710 ROE CREST DRIVE
NORTH MANKATO, MN 56003
WWW.CAPSTONEYOUNGREADERS.COM

CATALOGING-IN-PUBLICATION DATA IS AVAILABLE
ON THE LIBRARY OF CONGRESS WEBSITE.
ISBN: 978-1-4342-6021-5 (LIBRARY HARDCOVER)
ISBN: 978-1-4342-6191-5 (PAPERBACK)

PRINTED IN THE UNITED STATES OF AMERICA
IN STEVENS POINT, WISCONSIN.
082013   007666R

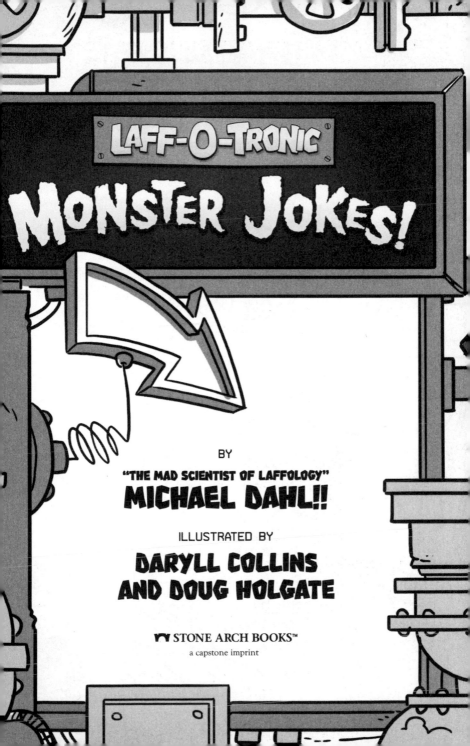

LAFF-O-TRONIC

MONSTER JOKES!

BY

"THE MAD SCIENTIST OF LAFFOLOGY"
MICHAEL DAHL!!

ILLUSTRATED BY

DARYLL COLLINS
AND DOUG HOLGATE

STONE ARCH BOOKS™
a capstone imprint

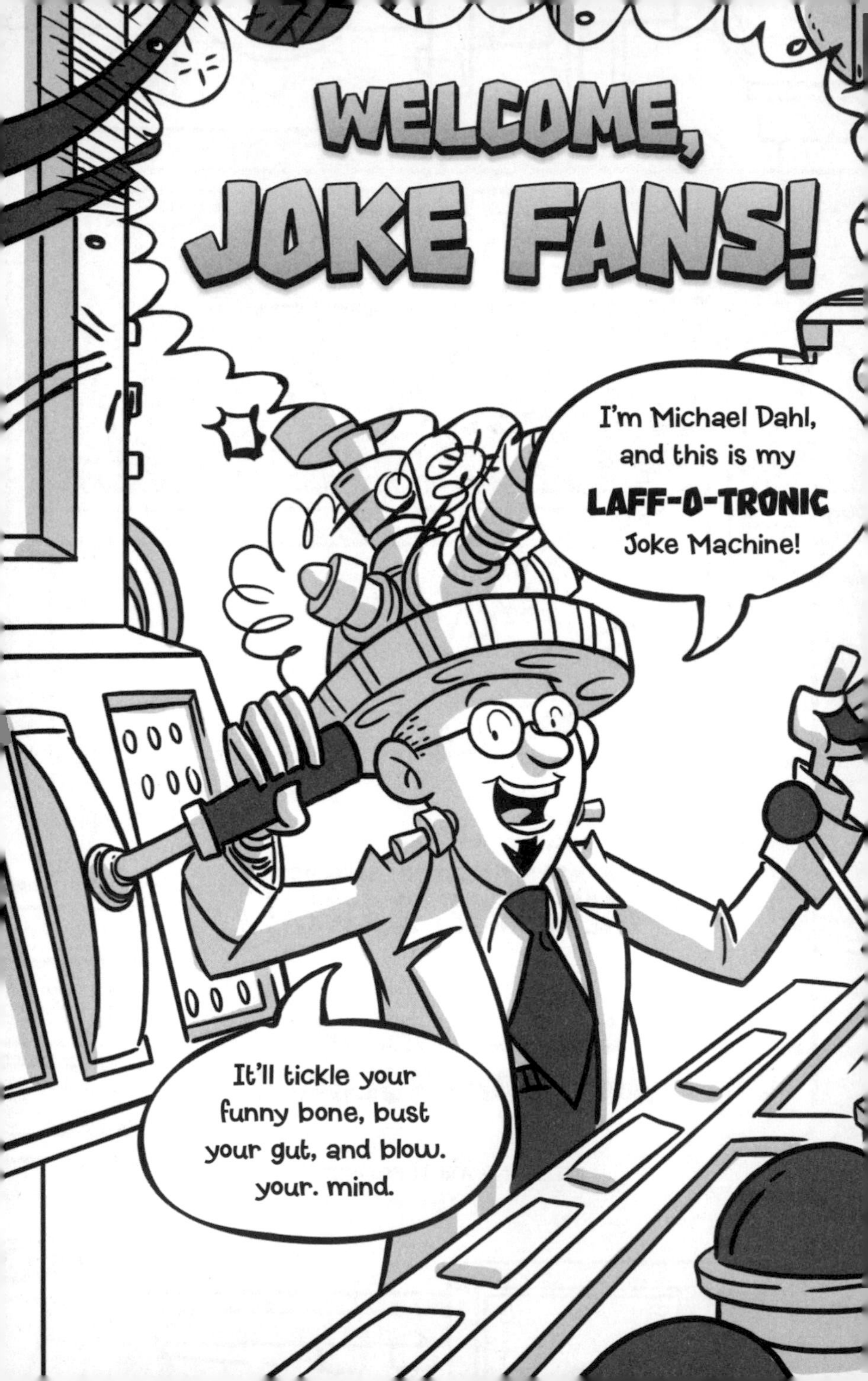
WELCOME, JOKE FANS!
I'm Michael Dahl, and this is my LAFF-O-TRONIC Joke Machine!
It'll tickle your funny bone, bust your gut, and blow. your. mind.

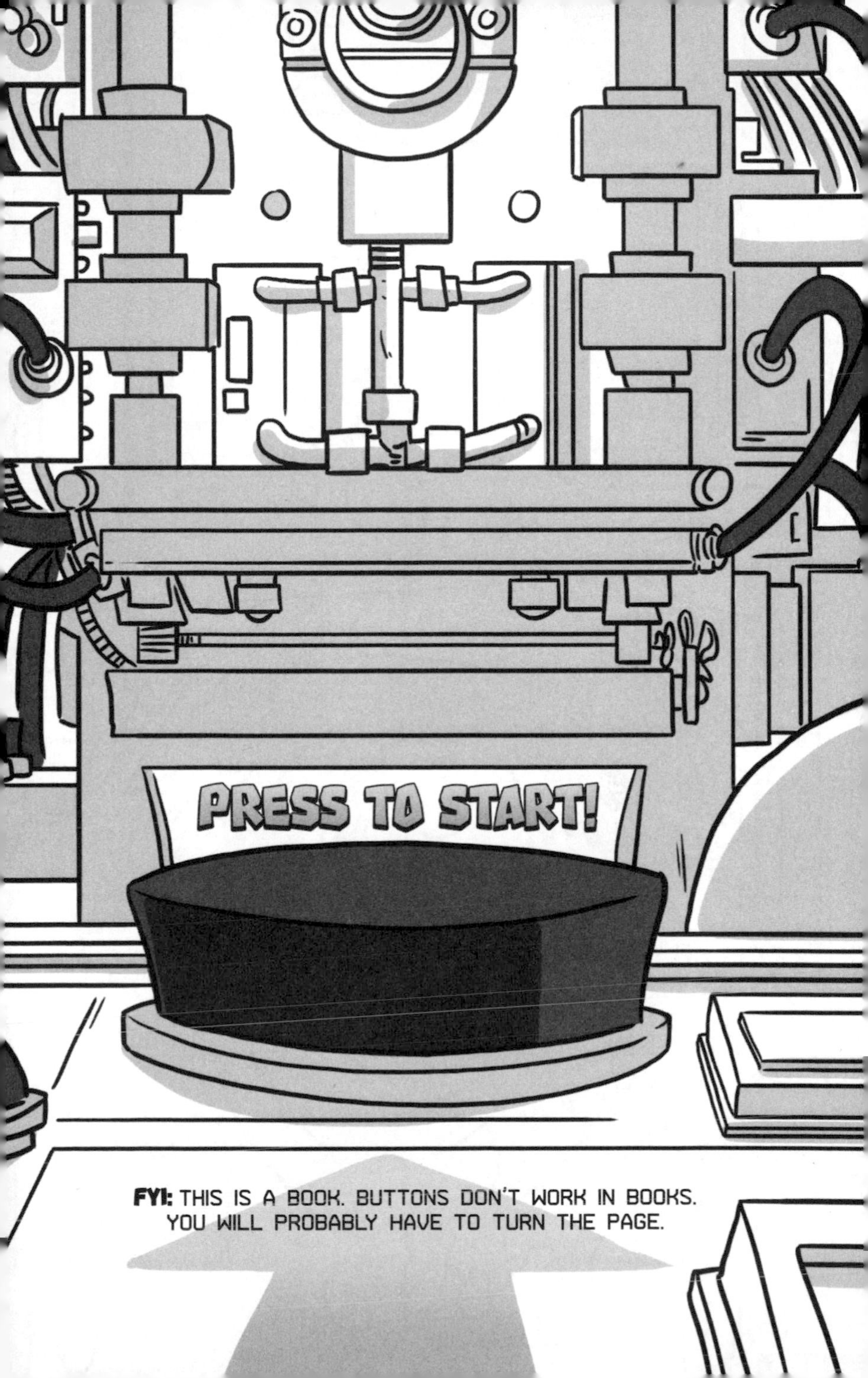
PRESS TO START!
FYI: THIS IS A BOOK. BUTTONS DON'T WORK IN BOOKS.
YOU WILL PROBABLY HAVE TO TURN THE PAGE.

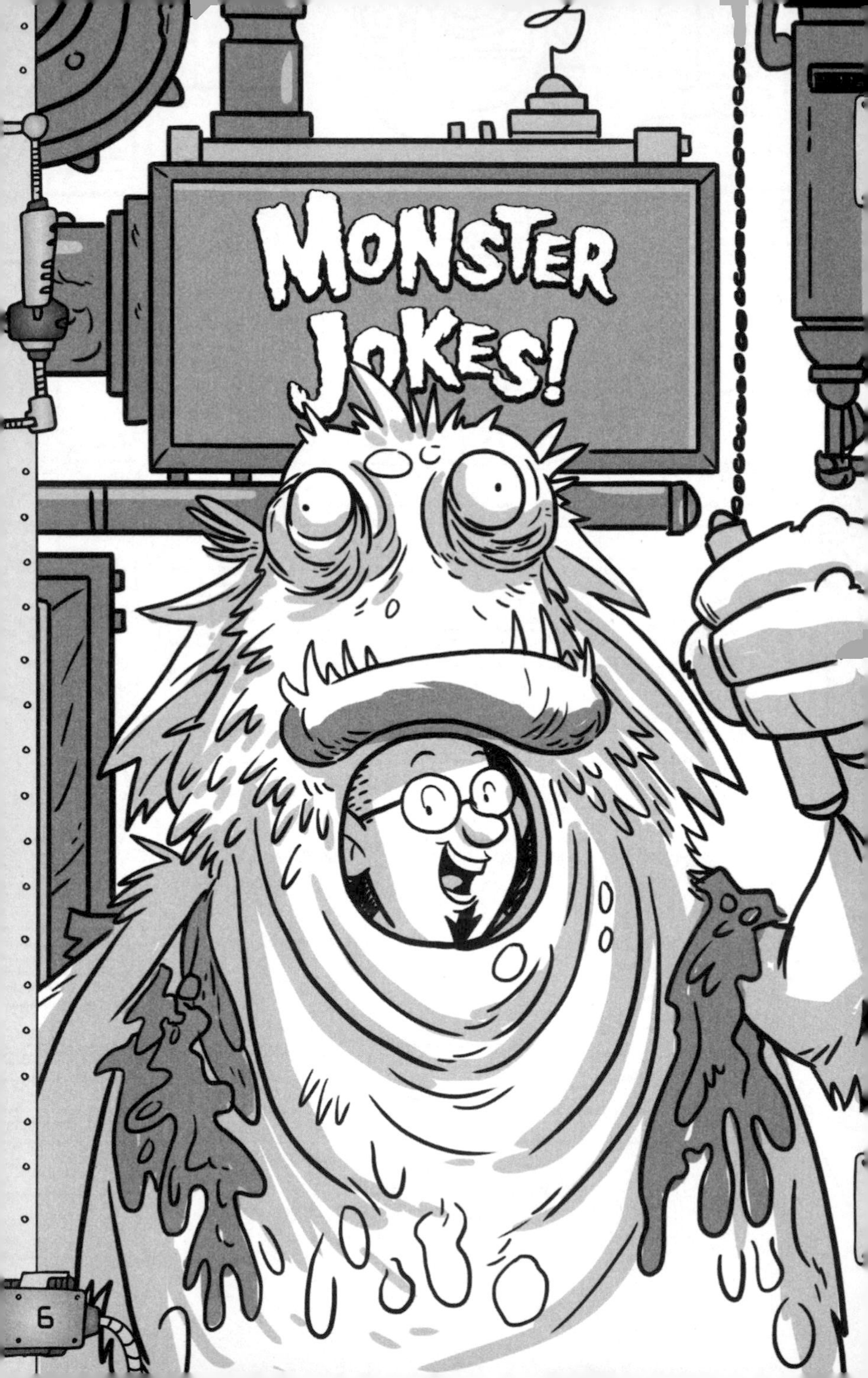
MONSTER JOKES!

You hear the Invisible Man has a girlfriend?
Yeah, but I just don't get what she sees in him.

Did you know the Invisible Man has kids?
Yeah, but they're nothing to look at.

Have you seen the Invisible Man's dog?
No.
That's funny, neither has he.

How do ghosts shave?
With shaving scream.

What did the sheet say to the ghost?
I got you covered.

Why don't skeletons play music in church?
They don't have any organs.

**What goes "Buzz buzz moan . . .
buzz buzz moan?"**
I give.
Zom-bees.

What is Dracula's favorite kind of pet?
A bloodhound.

Why are zombies terrible actors?
They give everyone else stage fright!

**What is the favorite book
of one-eyed monsters?**
The encyclops-edia.

What does a sad ghost say?
Boo-hoo!

**What position does a monster
play in soccer?**
Ghoulie.

**What happened when the monster ran
away with the circus?**
The police made him bring it back.

Why did Frankenstein eat the street lamp?
He wanted a light snack.

Why did the mummy need a vacation?
He was coming unraveled.

What's a mummy's favorite music?
Wrap.

What did the director say when he finished the mummy movie?
"It's a wrap!"

What's all that applause coming from the mad scientist's laboratory?
Oh, he's just giving Frankenstein a hand.

Why didn't the zombie eat the clown?

Because he tasted funny.

What do sea monsters eat?

Fish and ships!

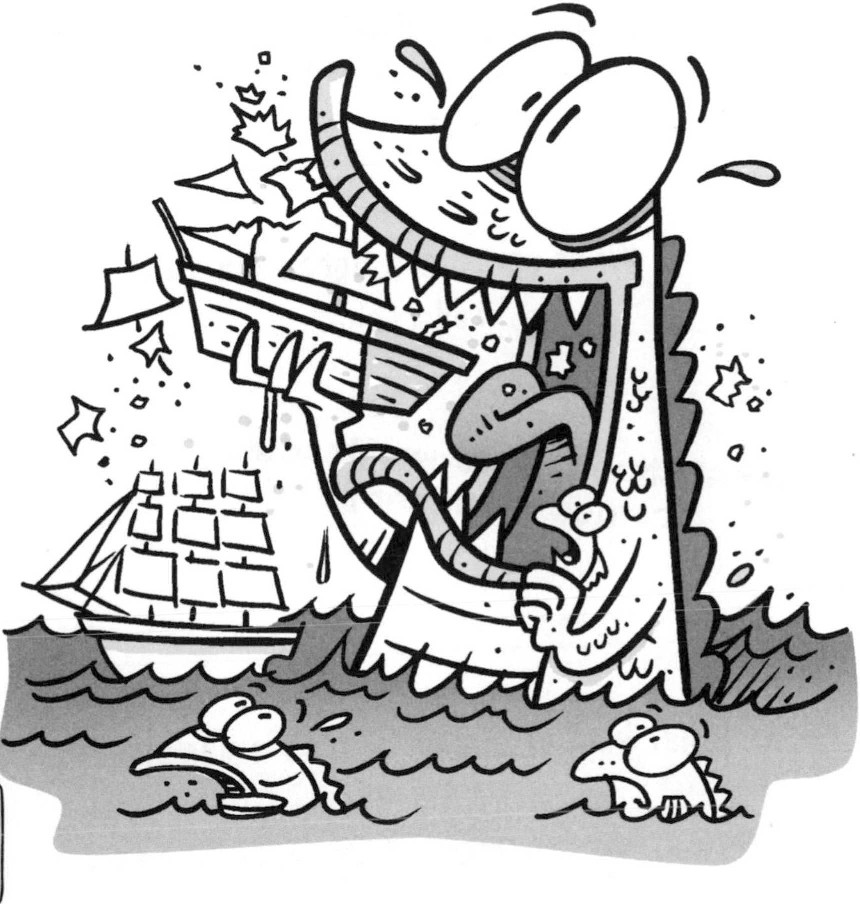

What monster wears a mask and has a long gray trunk?

The Elephantom of the Opera!

What do you call a zombie with lots of kids?

A momster.

What sport are ogres good at?

Troller-skating.

What time is it when Dracula comes to dinner?

Time to leave!

What kind of dinner scares a vampire?

Steak!

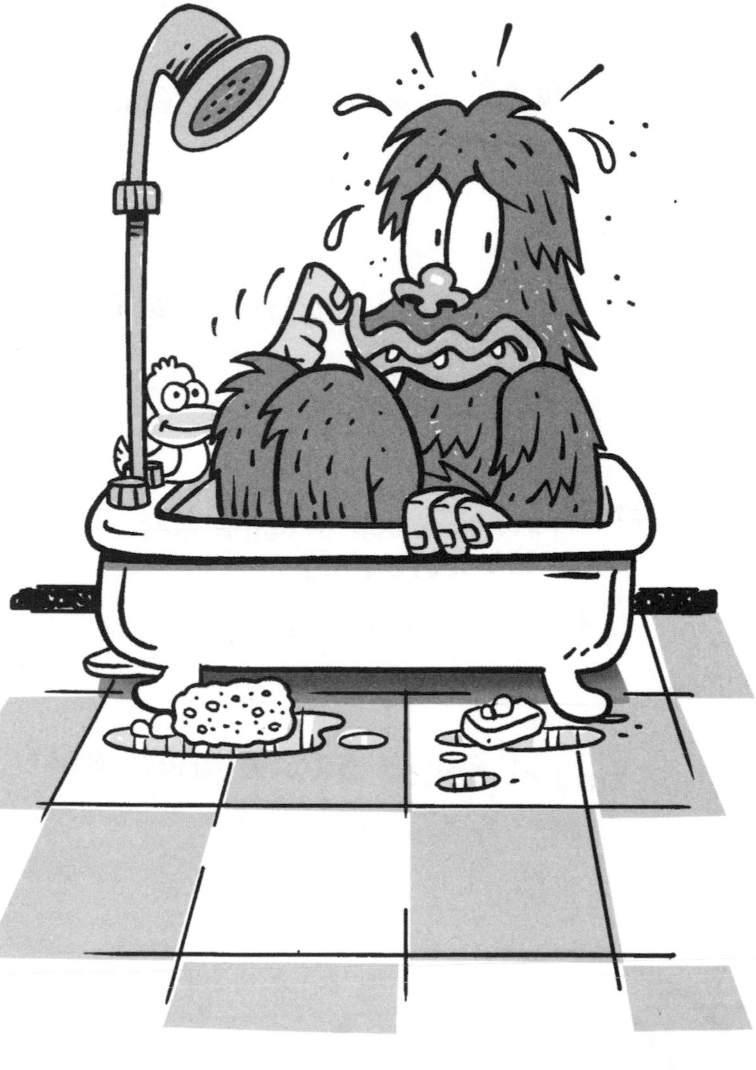

What do you call Bigfoot in a bathtub?

Stuck.

Why do you address Dracula as "Count"?
Because if you don't, your days are numbered!

How do you contact the Kraken?
Drop it a line.

What happened when Dracula met the Werewolf?
They fought tooth and nail!

What kind of pasta did the ghost eat?
Spook-etti.

Why are there fences around cemeteries?

Because everyone is dying to get in!

What do you say to a two-headed monster?

Hello and hello.

What side of Godzilla's mouth has the sharpest teeth?

The inside!

What do you find between Godzilla's toes?

Slow runners.

Why did the Invisible Man look in the mirror?

To see if he wasn't there.

TONS-O-TOONS!

"I just came from the beauty salon."

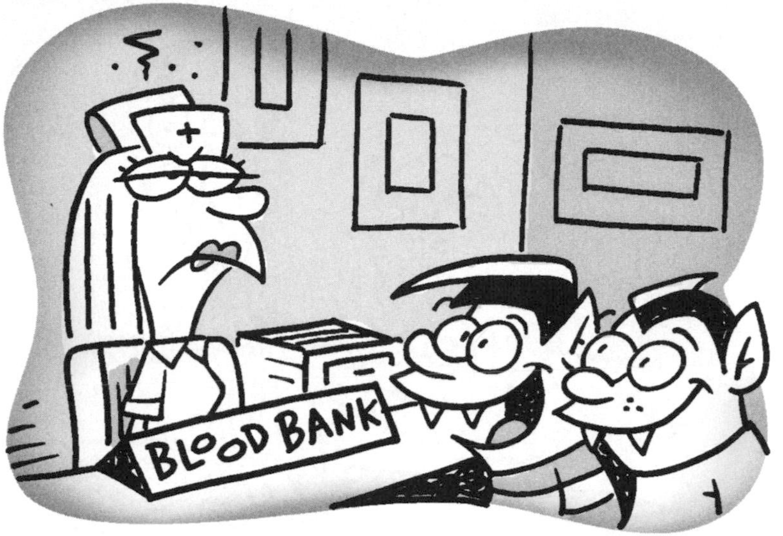
BLOOD BANK

VAMPIRE: "We'd like to make a withdrawal."

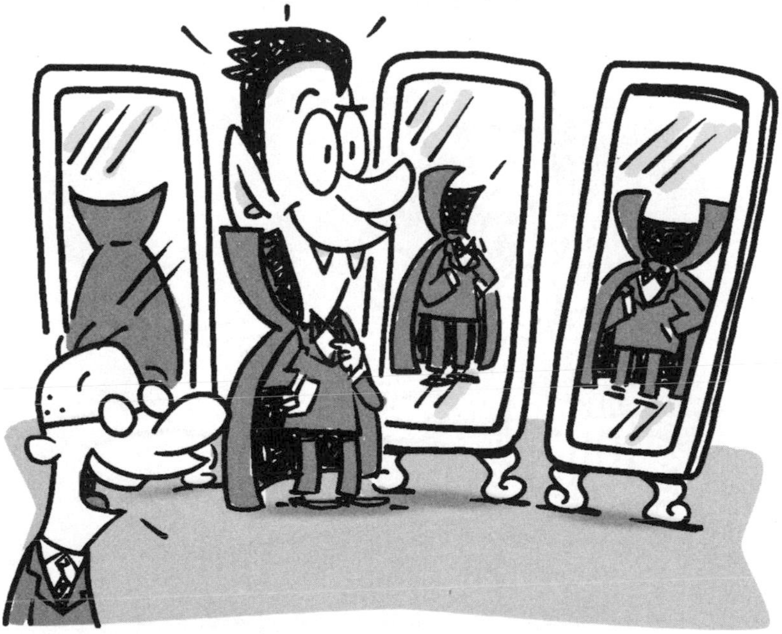

STORE CLERK: "You never looked better!"

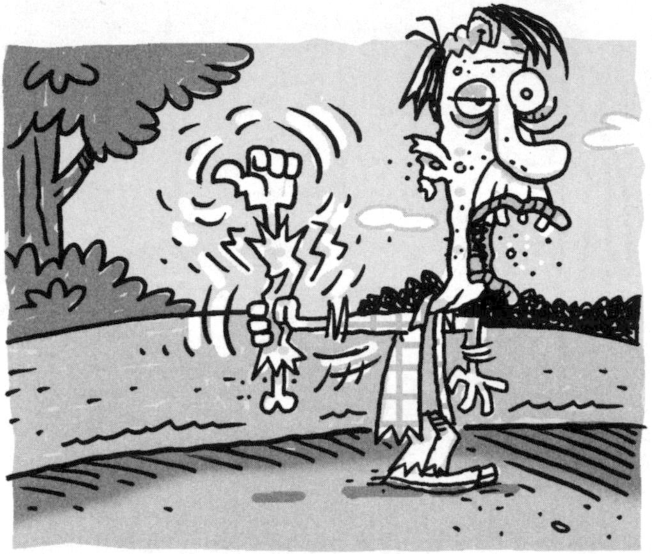

Zombie hitchhiker.

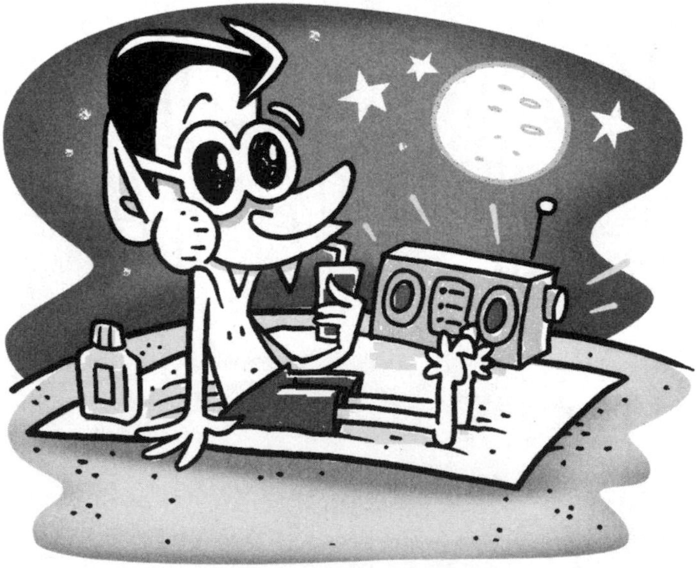

A night at the beach.

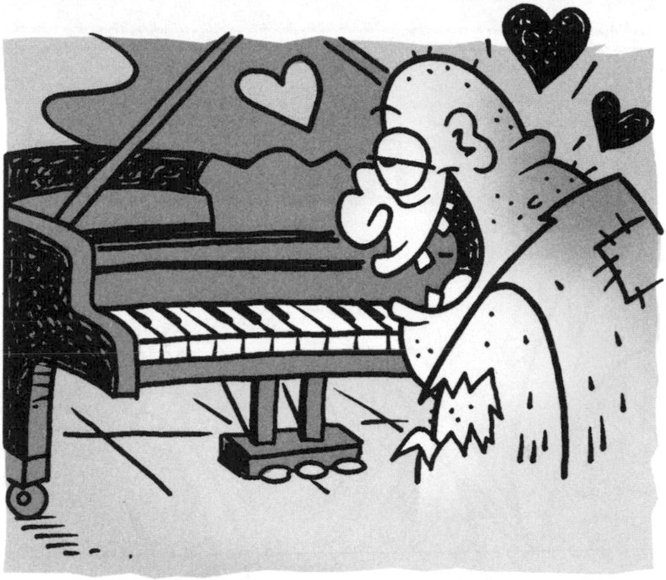

Monster: "You have a lovely smile!"

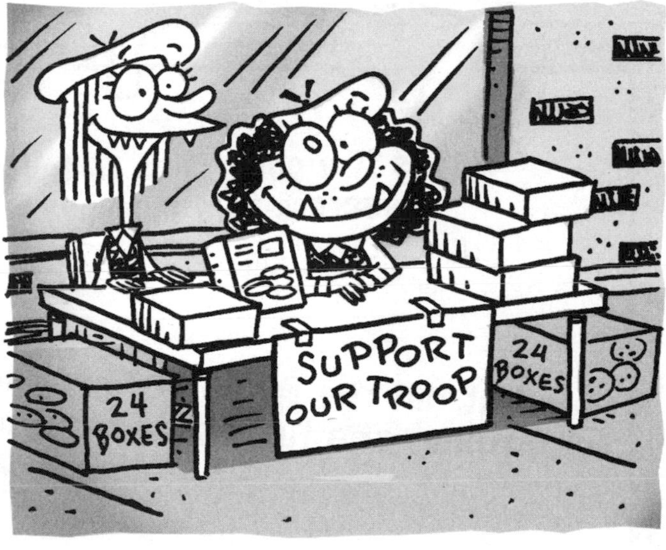
SUPPORT OUR TROOP
24 BOXES
24 BOXES

Ghoul Scout Cookies

MORE JOKES!

Why is it a good thing to tell your secrets to a mummy?

He'll always keep it under wraps.

What did the Bride of Frankenstein say when she first saw the monster?

"It's love at first fright!"

Why don't skeletons like to bungee jump?
Because they don't have the guts!

**Why wasn't any food left over
at the monster party?**
Because everyone was a goblin!

What do you call a sticky mummy?
Gummy.

**Do zombies eat popcorn with
their fingers?**
No, they eat the fingers separately.

What kind of hot dogs do monsters eat?
Hallo-weiners.

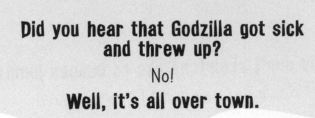

Did you hear that Godzilla got sick and threw up?

No!

Well, it's all over town.

Why are ghosts so good at hearing things?
Because they are ear-y!

Why did the Cyclops quit teaching?
He only had one pupil.

Why did the little monster buy three socks?
Because she grew another foot.

Who did the zombie boy take to the prom?
His ghoul friend.

What kind of witch is good to have with you in the dark?
A lights witch!

Monster: "Where do fleas go in the winter?"
Werewolf: "Search me!"

What do little vampires eat?
Alpha-bat soup!

What is an alien monster's favorite game?
Swallow the leader!

What do you call a spooky wizard?
Scary Potter!

What do you get when Dracula is your teacher?
Lots of blood tests!

What did the grandmother monster say to her grandson when he came to visit?

"You gruesome!"

What did the little zombie take to bed?

Her deady bear.

What do you call a friendly mummy?

Chummy.

How do you know when there's a monster under your bed?

If your nose touches the ceiling!

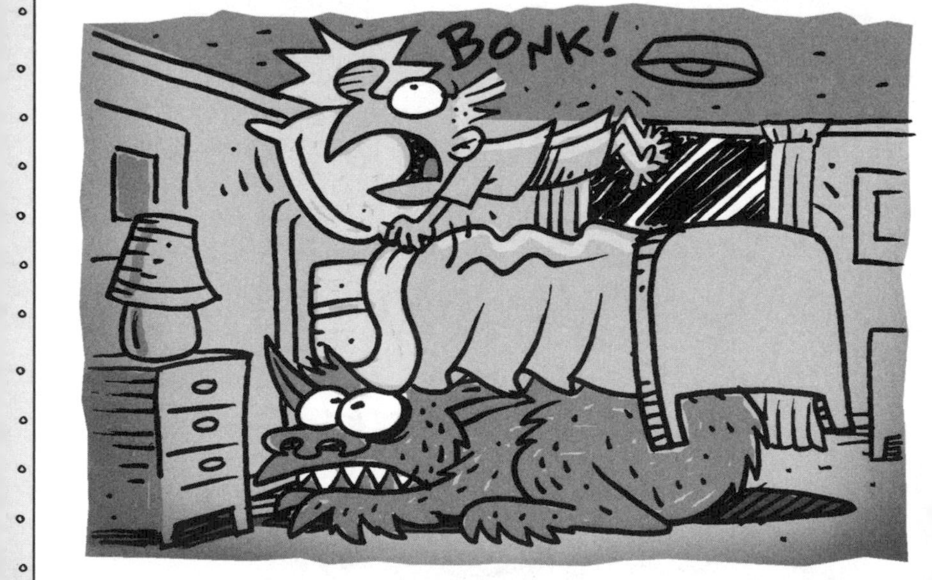
BONK!

What did one vampire say to the other vampire?

"Is that you coffin?"

What did the skeleton musician play?

A trombone!

When does a werewolf eat dinner?

Chewsday.

What do you get when you cross a snowman with a vampire?

Frostbite!

Why wasn't the mad scientist ever lonely?

Because he was so good at making new friends.

What did the polite monster say to the man?

"Pleased to eat you!"

Why do you need a dictionary when you talk to a giant?

Because you have to use BIG words!

What should you do if zombies crash through your front door?

Run out the back one!

Why didn't the Swamp Monster go to the party after school?

He got bogged down in his homework.

What did the dragon say when it cornered the knight?

"You're toast!"

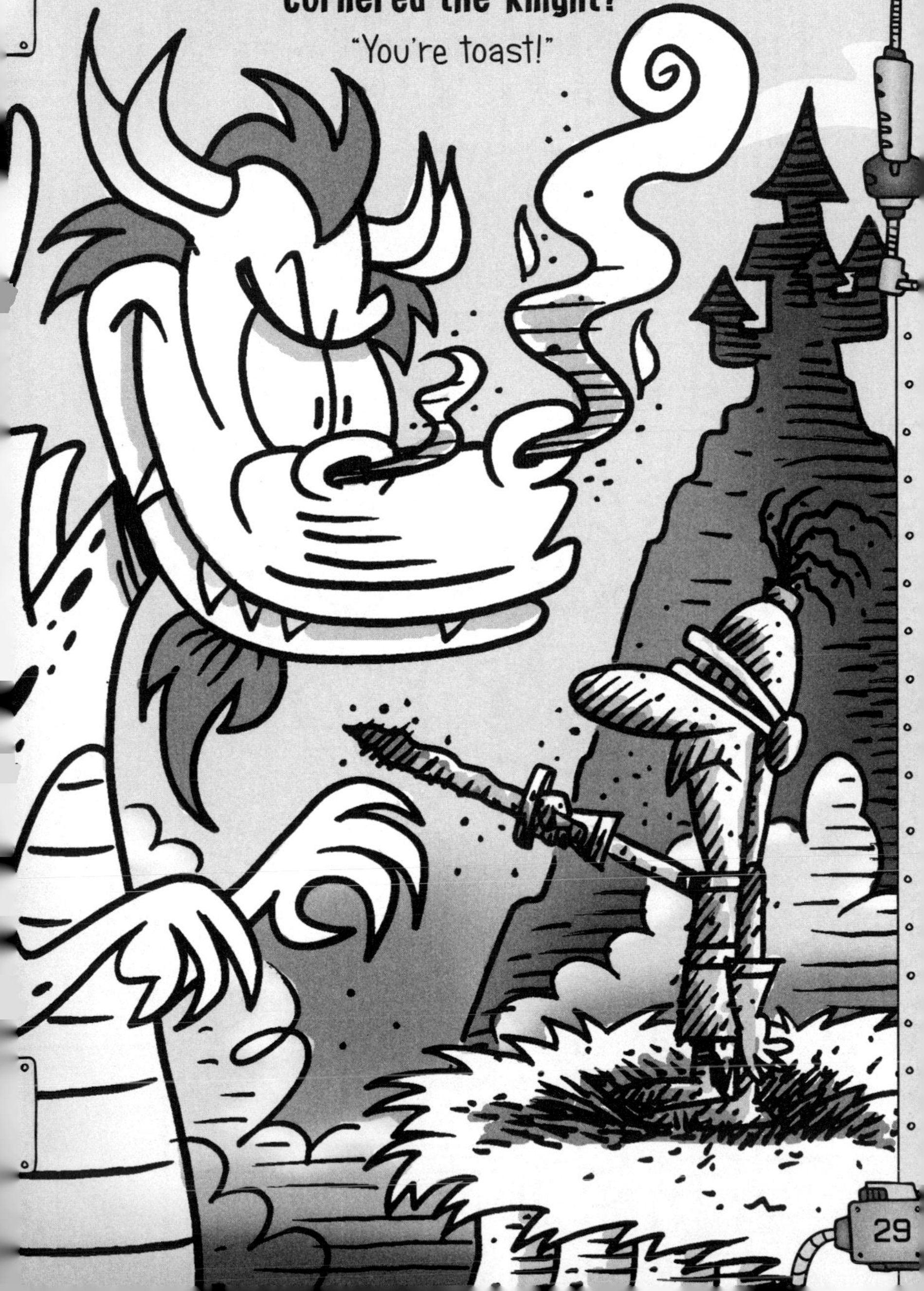

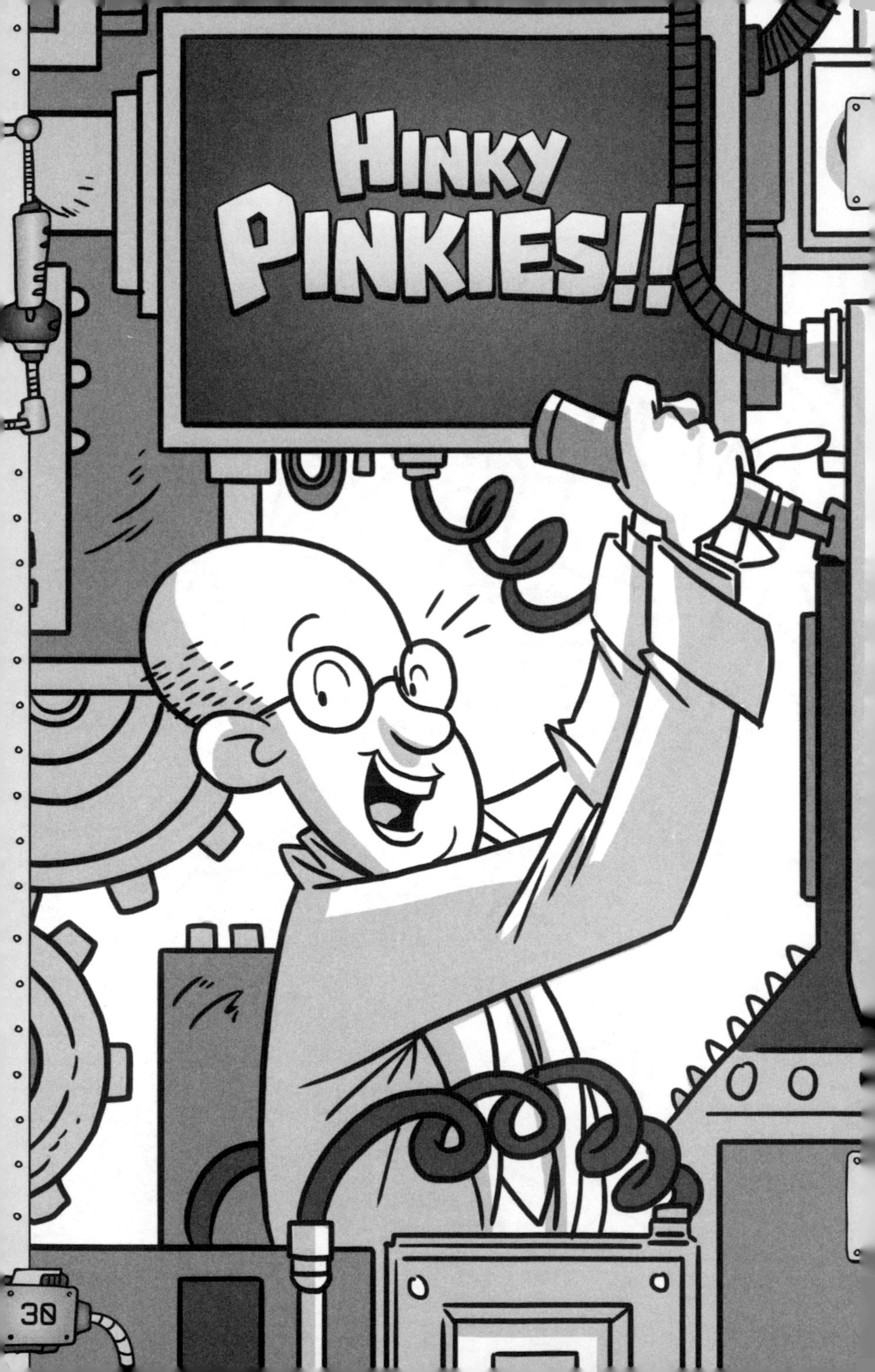
HINKY PINKIES!!

What do you call a magician who works with reptiles?

A LIZARD WIZARD

What do you call a giant ape that breathes fire and attacks the city of Tokyo?

GORILLA GODZILLA

What kind of sneakers does a one-eyed monster wear?

CYCLOPS HIGH-TOPS

What do you call a dead pharaoh who's been playing with glue?

A GUMMY MUMMY

What do you call the Abominable Snowman after his exercise workout?

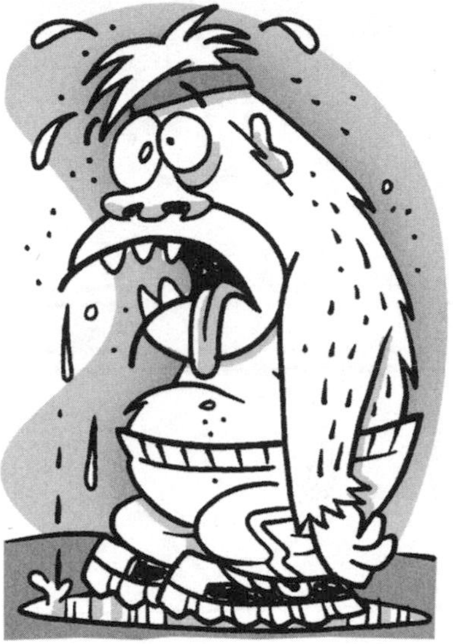

A SWEATY YETI

What special fee do ogres have to pay when driving on the road?

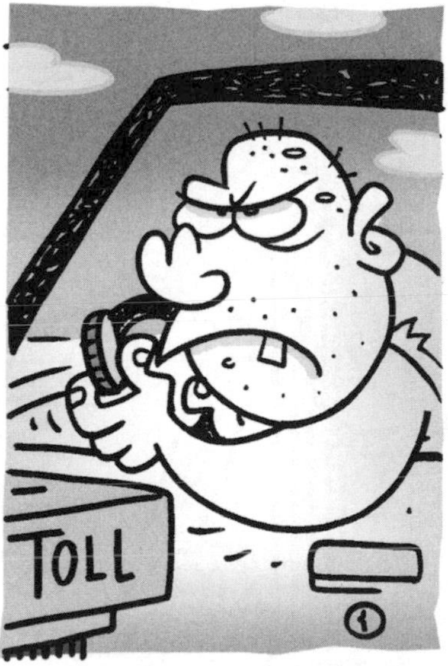
TOLL

A TROLL TOLL

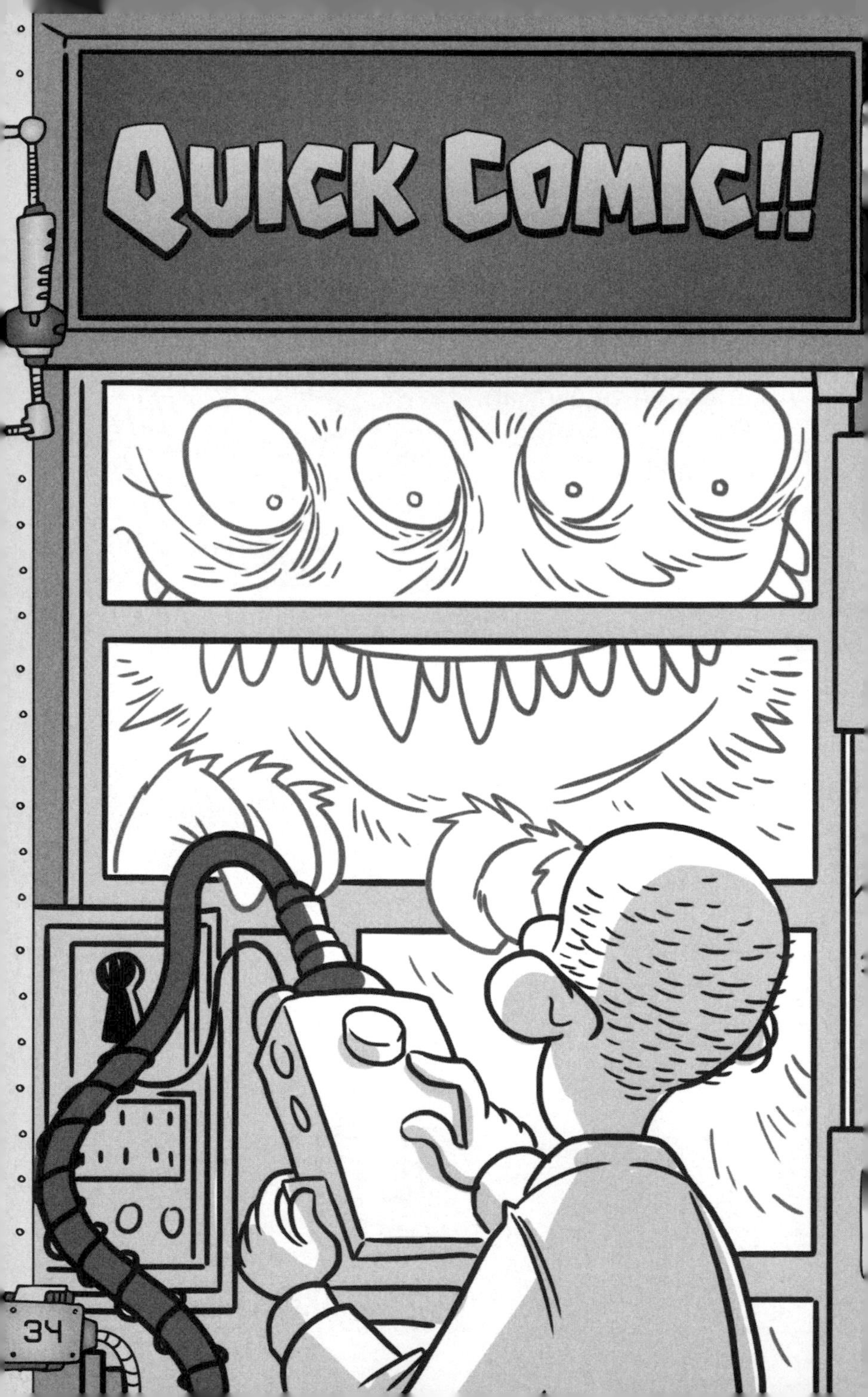
QUICK COMIC!!
34

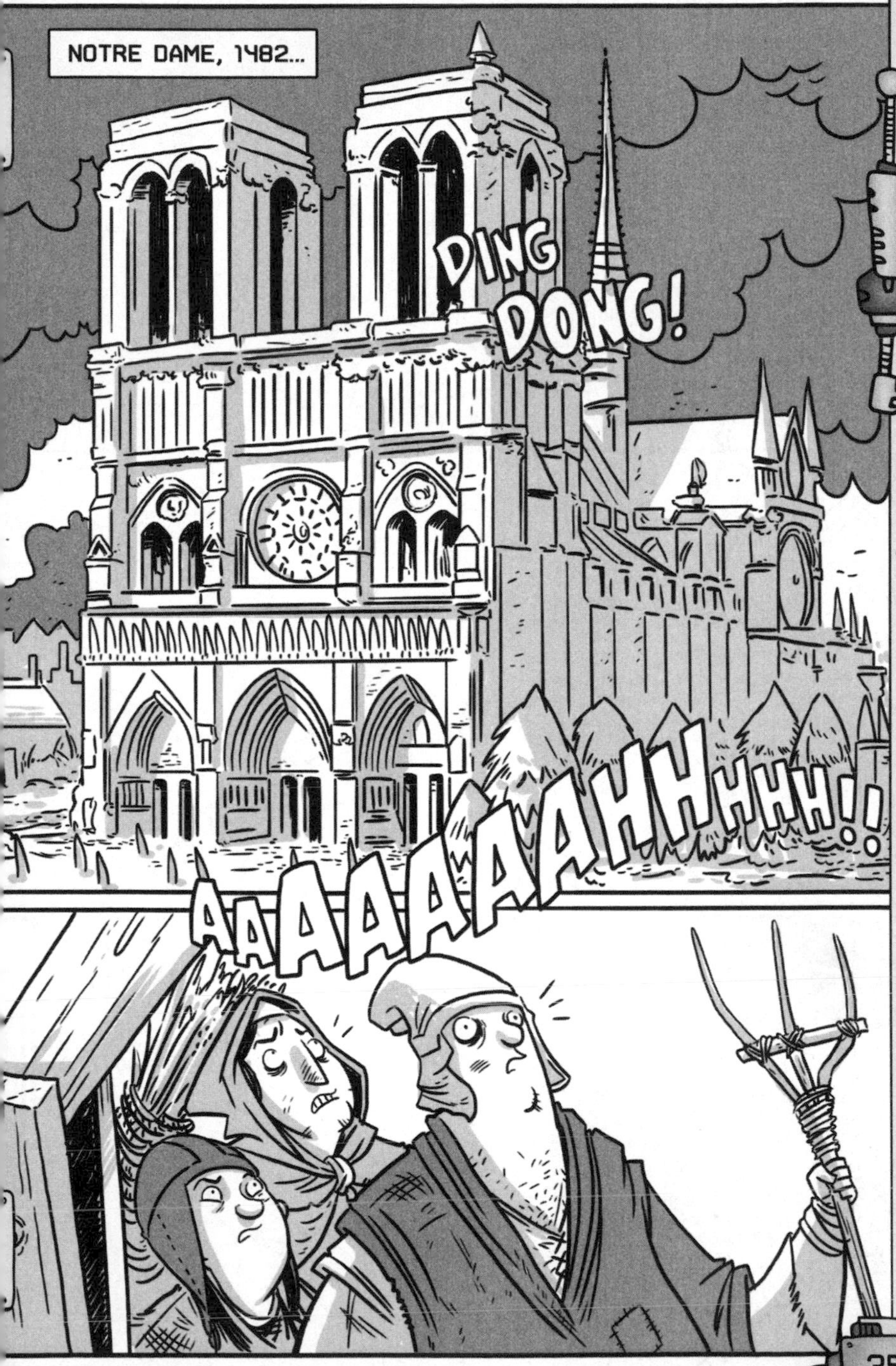
NOTRE DAME, 1482...
DING DONG!
AAAAAAAAHHHHHH!!

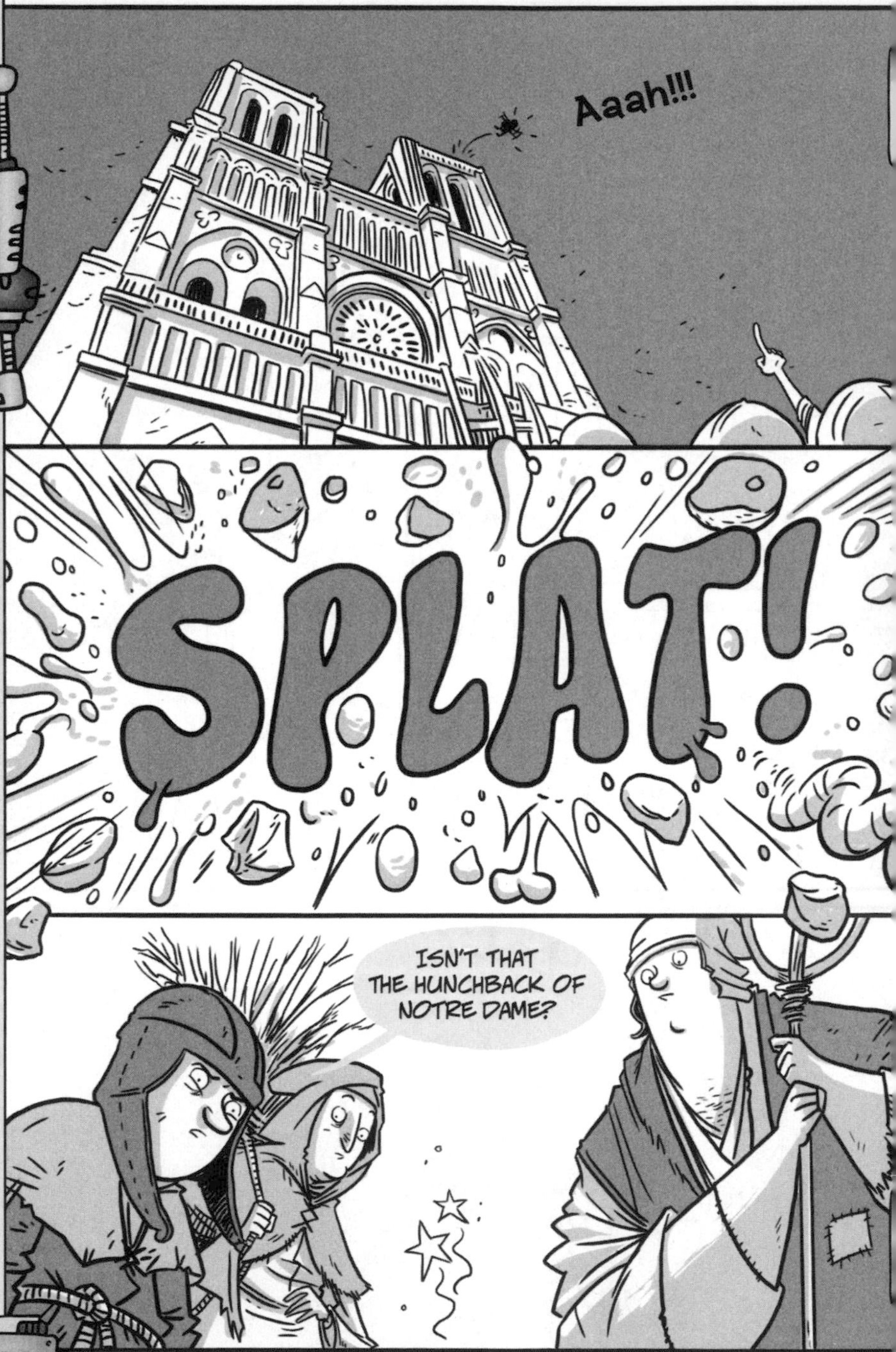
Aaah!!!
SPLAT!
ISN'T THAT THE HUNCHBACK OF NOTRE DAME?

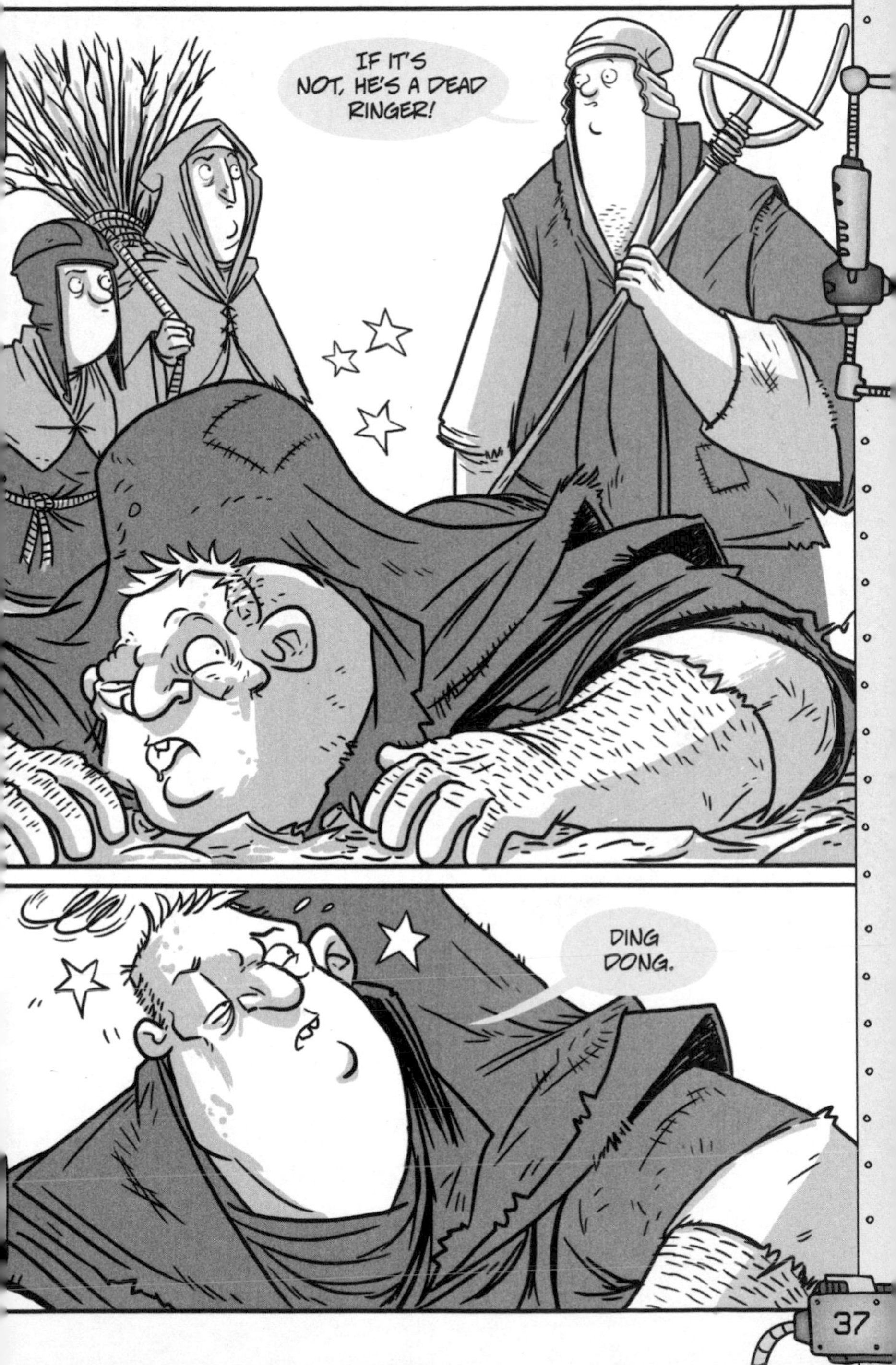
IF IT'S NOT, HE'S A DEAD RINGER!
DING DONG.

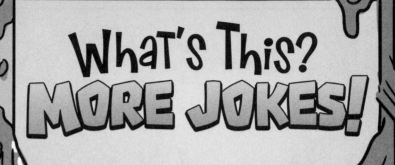

What's This? MORE JOKES!

What did Godzilla say when the town caught on fire?

"Barbecue!"

What does the Headless Horseman ride?

A night-mare!

When do werewolves make the loudest racket?
On Moon-day.

I heard the Wolfman got a great job.
Yes, he's a hair-traffic controller.

Why did the zombie carry a handbag?
To carry all her extra hands.

Why was the female zombie at the party?
She was looking for an edible bachelor!

What time is it when a monster sits on your car?

Time to get a new car!

What do you call Bigfoot's family?

Bigfeet.

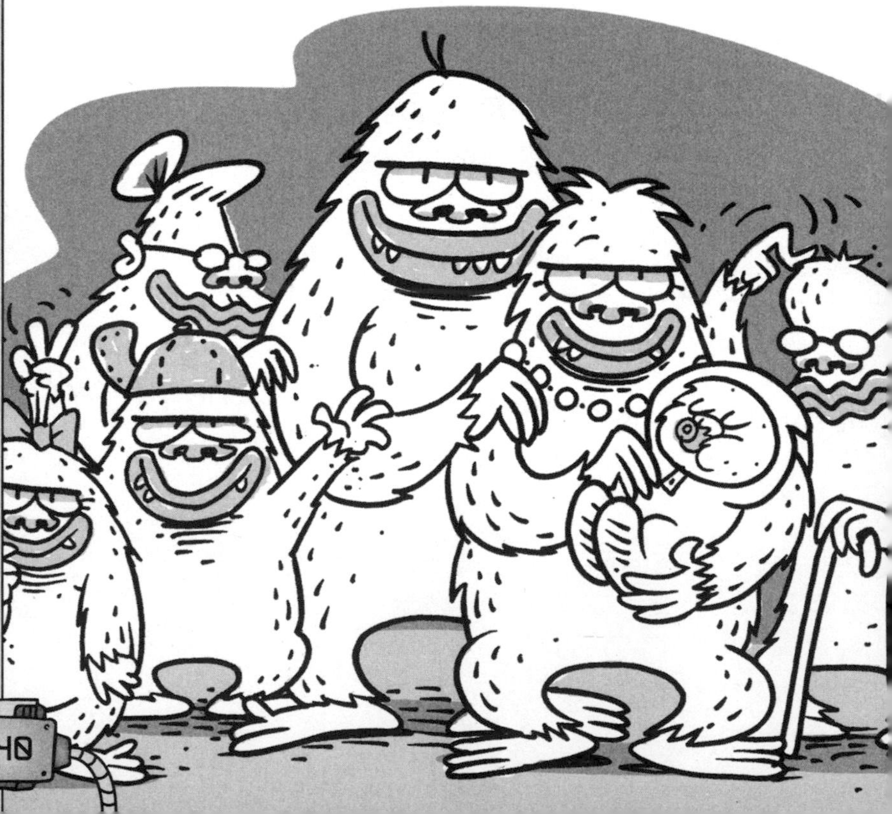

What's big and hairy and climbs up the Empire State Building in a dress?

Queen Kong!

Why did King Kong join the army?

To learn gorilla warfare!

Why don't mummies ever go hungry in the desert?

Because of all the sand which is there.
(sandwiches there)

How does Dracula stay clean?

He jumps in the bat tub!

Why does the Mummy stay late at the office every night?

He's wrapped up in his work.

What's a vampire's favorite sport?

Batminton.

Why is the Abominable Snowman so popular?

'Cause he's cool!

What do you call a skeleton with a broom?

The Grim Sweeper.

Why couldn't the Werewolf run in the marathon?

He wasn't part of the human race.

What's the best way to talk to an alien creature?

From far away!

Why doesn't Dracula have any friends?

Because he's a pain in the neck!

What did the Loch Ness Monster say to his friend?

"Long time no sea!"

What do you get if you cross a Scottish sea monster with a shark?

Loch Jaws!

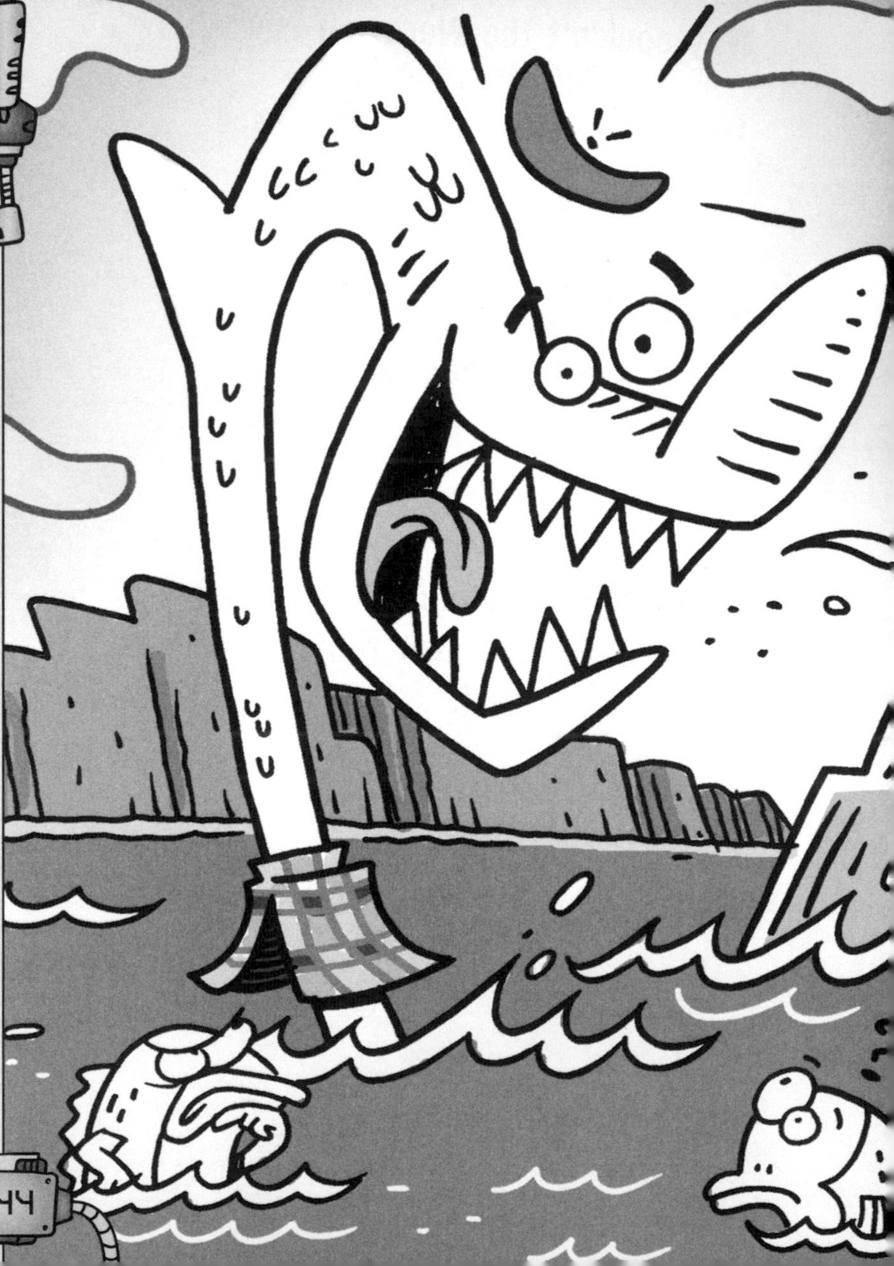

Why did the ghost go to the doctor?
Because it came down with the boo-bonic plague!

**Why did the vampire
become a pop singer?**
It was in his blood!

Why didn't Godzilla eat the hotel?
He was trying to cut down on suites.

**Did you hear about the two
vampires who raced each other?**
Yeah, they finished neck and neck.

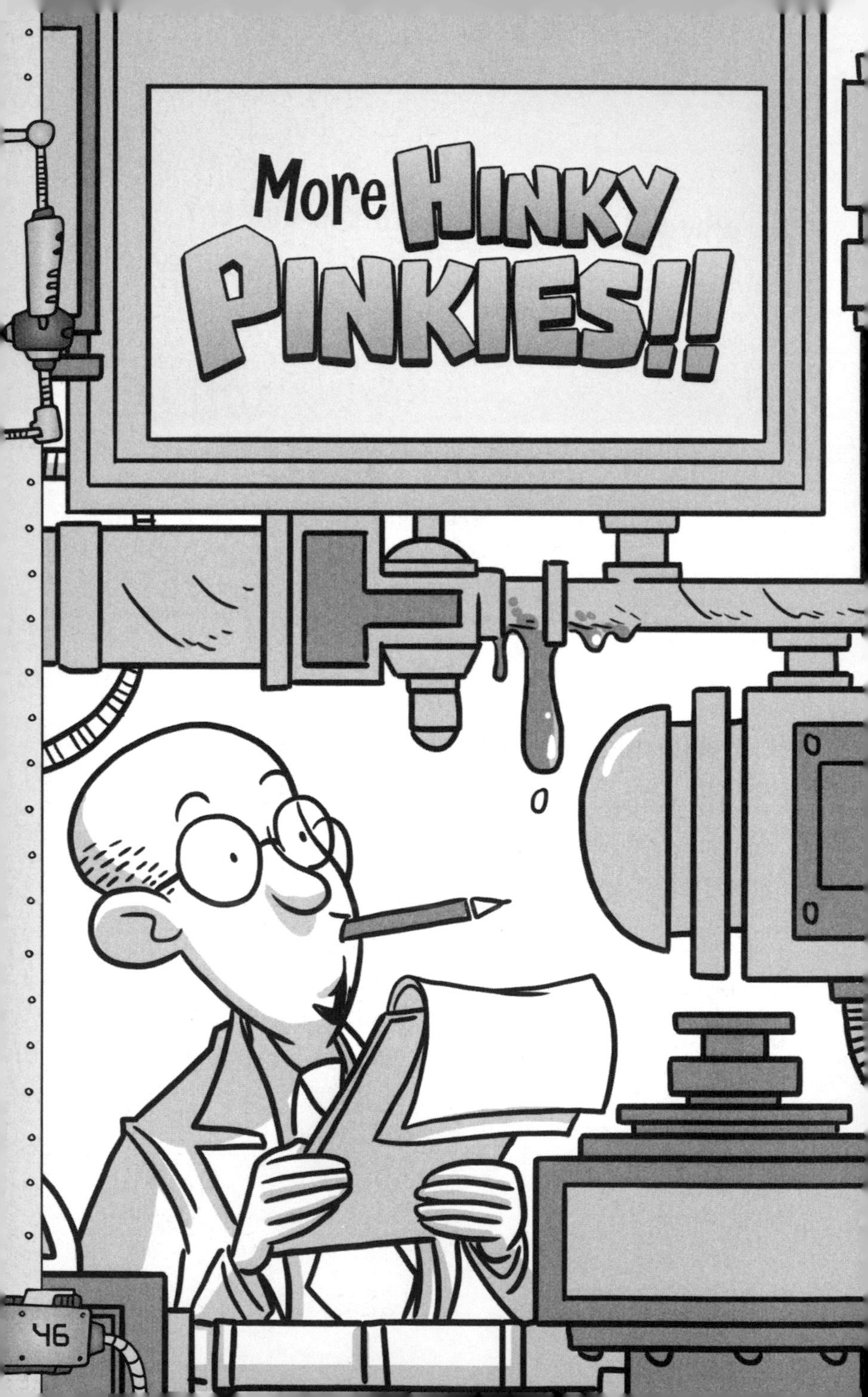
More HINKY PINKIES!!

What does a
zombie call a dead
Egyptian that
tastes good?

A YUMMY MUMMY!

What do you call a
goblin that works
for the Russian
government?

A KREMLIN GREMLIN

What does a baby
fire-breathing monster
like to ride in?

A DRAGON WAGON

What do you call a big
dance in a cemetery?

A GRAVE RAVE

What does an ogre from Middle-Earth use to eat spaghetti?

AN ORC FORK

What do you call a creature made of bones and gelatin?

A GELATIN SKELETON!

TONS-O-TOONS!

Monster: "Wow! That painting is hideous!
Art Patron: "It's a mirror."

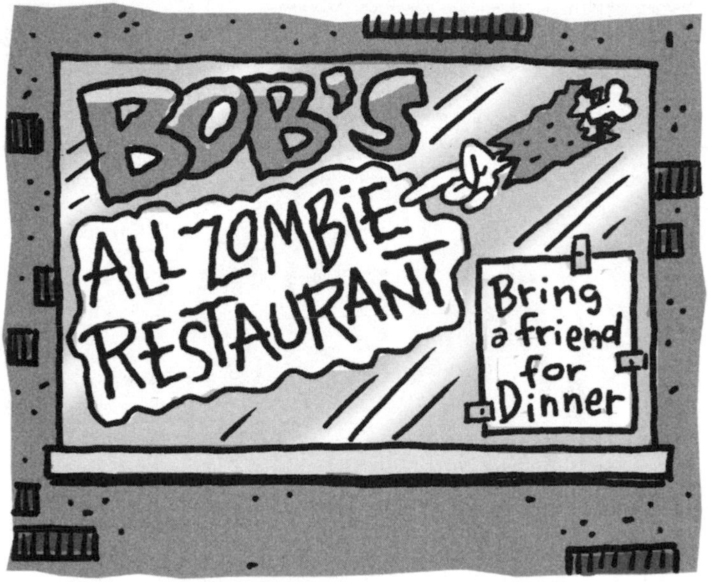
BOB'S
ALL ZOMBIE RESTAURANT
Bring a friend for Dinner

Bring a friend for dinner.

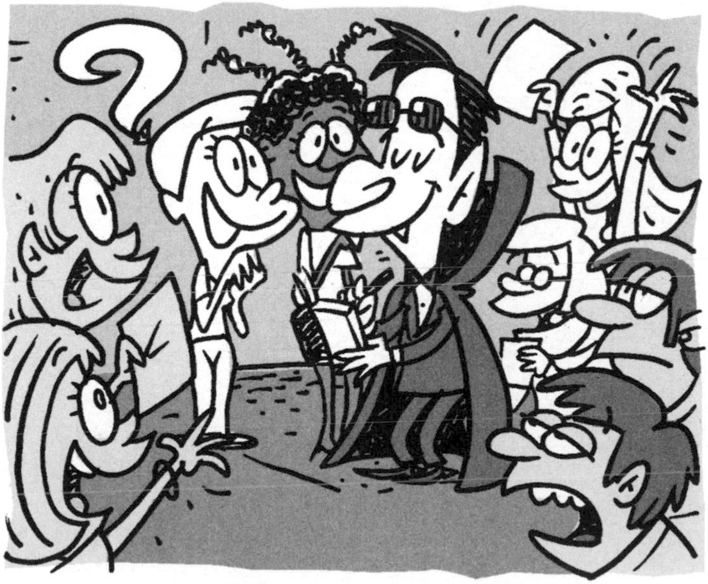

"Must be his fang club."

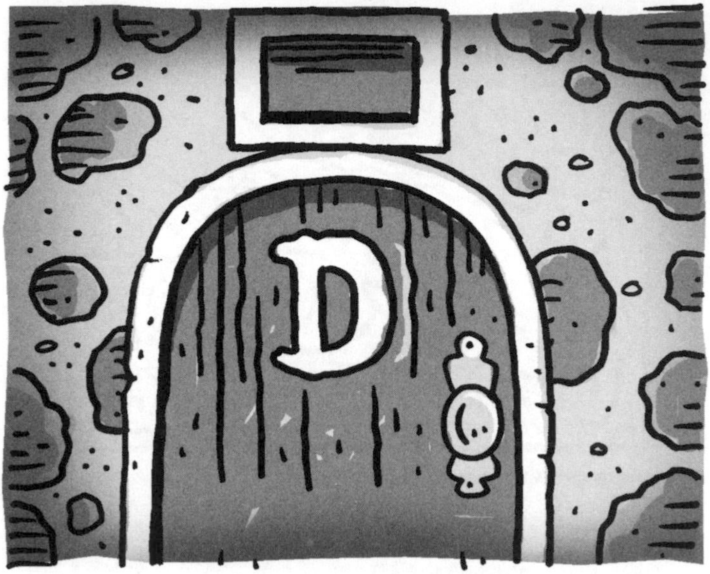
D

DRACULA'S PET DOOR.

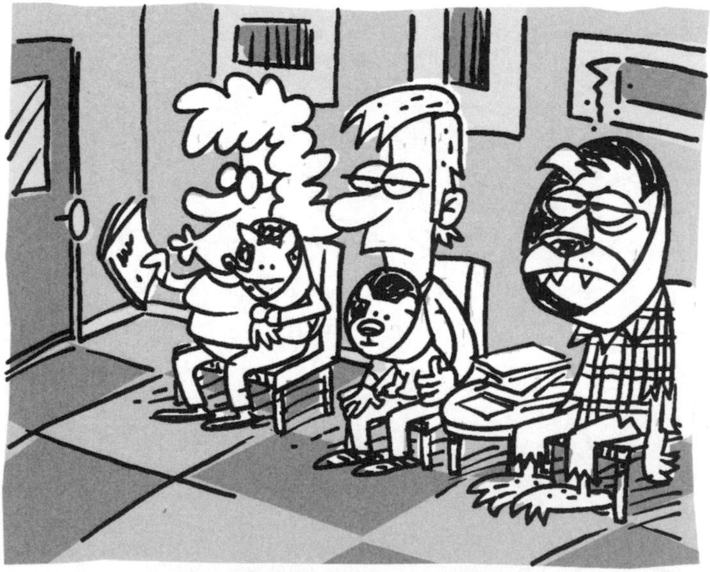

A DAY AT THE VET.

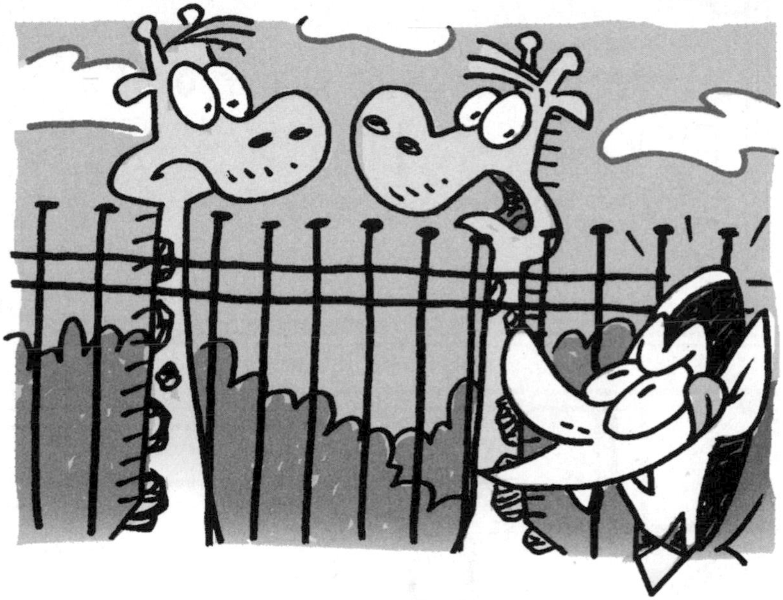

Giraffe: "I hate it when he looks at me like that!"

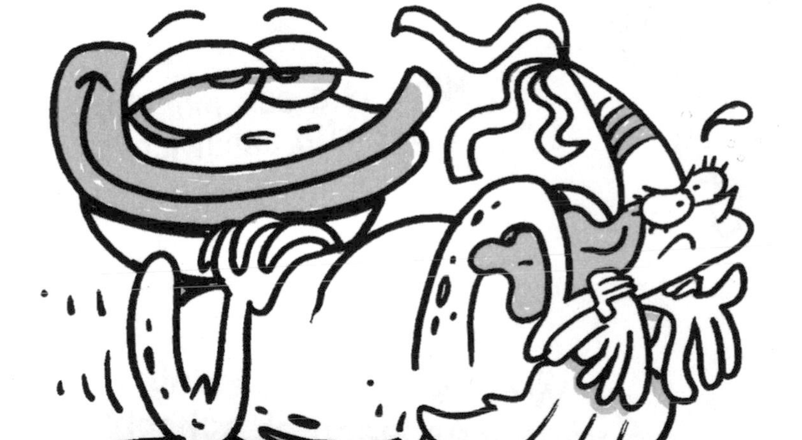

Lady: "He didn't turn into a prince. He just got king-sized!"

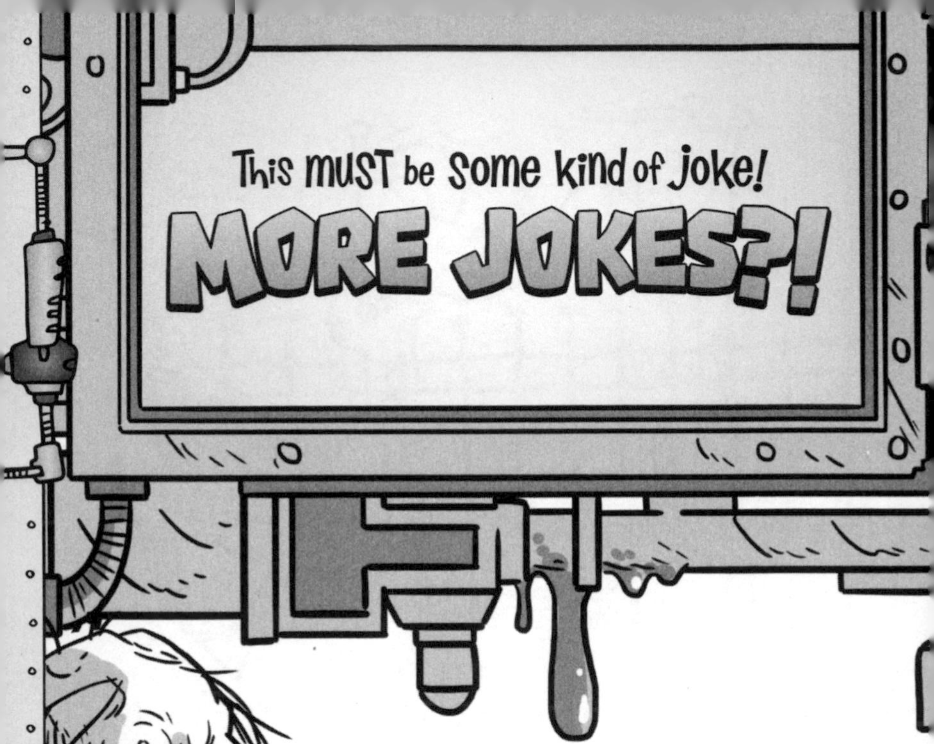

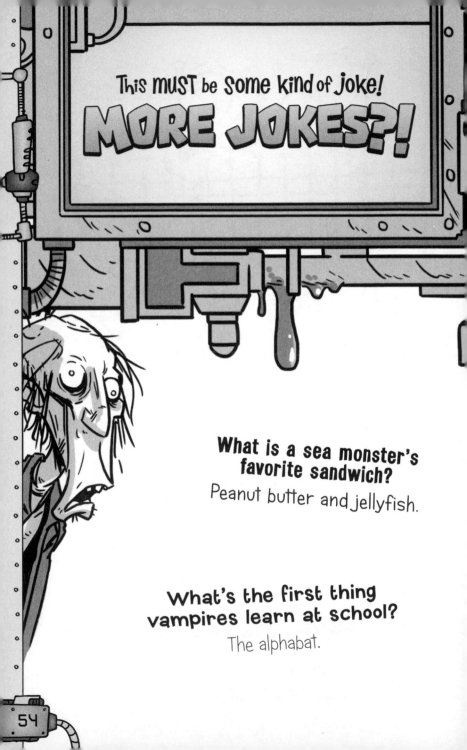

This MUST be some kind of joke!

MORE JOKES?!

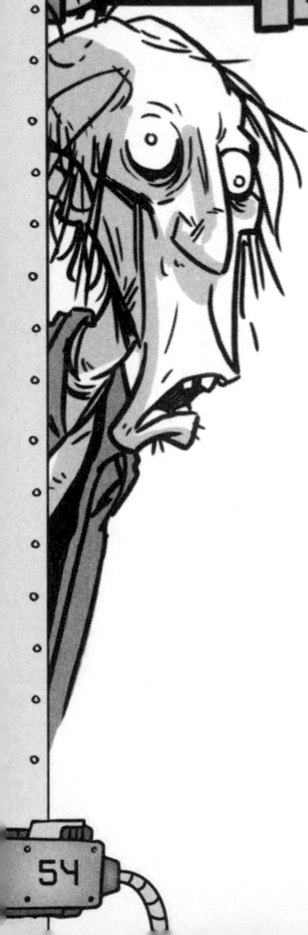

What is a sea monster's favorite sandwich?

Peanut butter and jellyfish.

What's the first thing vampires learn at school?

The alphabat.

What did the little vampire have for lunch?

Scream of tomato soup and a neck-tarine.

Why is Godzilla always so tired on the first of April?

Because he just had a march of 31 days!

What do you get if you cross a vampire with Sir Lancelot?

A bite in shining armor.

What do you get when Bigfoot walks through your garden?

Squash!

What did the scarecrow say when he was offered dessert?

"No thanks. I'm stuffed."

Where do zombies go swimming?

The Dead Sea.

What kind of plant grows only on Halloween?
Bam-BOO!

What do zombie kids eat for lunch?
Heads of lettuce and whole brain muffins.

Why did the policeman give the ghost a ticket?
Because he didn't have a haunting license.

How do you keep a vampire from biting his nails?
Replace the coffin nails with screws!

What's the most dangerous monster at the North Pole?

Yak the Ripper.

Why did the Monster from the Black Lagoon go to the hospital?

He was looking a little green.

What did a famous green ogre build on the back of his house?

A Shrek deck.

What do you hear if a giant ape rings your doorbell?

A King Kong ding-dong!

What do you call a giant ape playing table tennis?

Ping-Pong King Kong.

What do phantoms eat for breakfast?

Ghost toast.

What do you call the spooky leader of a church?

A Sinister minister.

Did you hear Frankenstein's going to medical school?

No, what's he studying?

The doctors are studying him!

King Kong: "I have to stomp twenty miles to the next town."

Godzilla: "Why don't you take the train?"

King Kong: "Because the last time I did that, my mom made me give it back!"

Mother: "Don't go swimming in the water. There are monsters out there!"

Boy: "But Dad's swimming out there."

Mom: "That's different—he's insured."

What do you call it when Godzilla has gas after a big meal?

A BURP-quake!

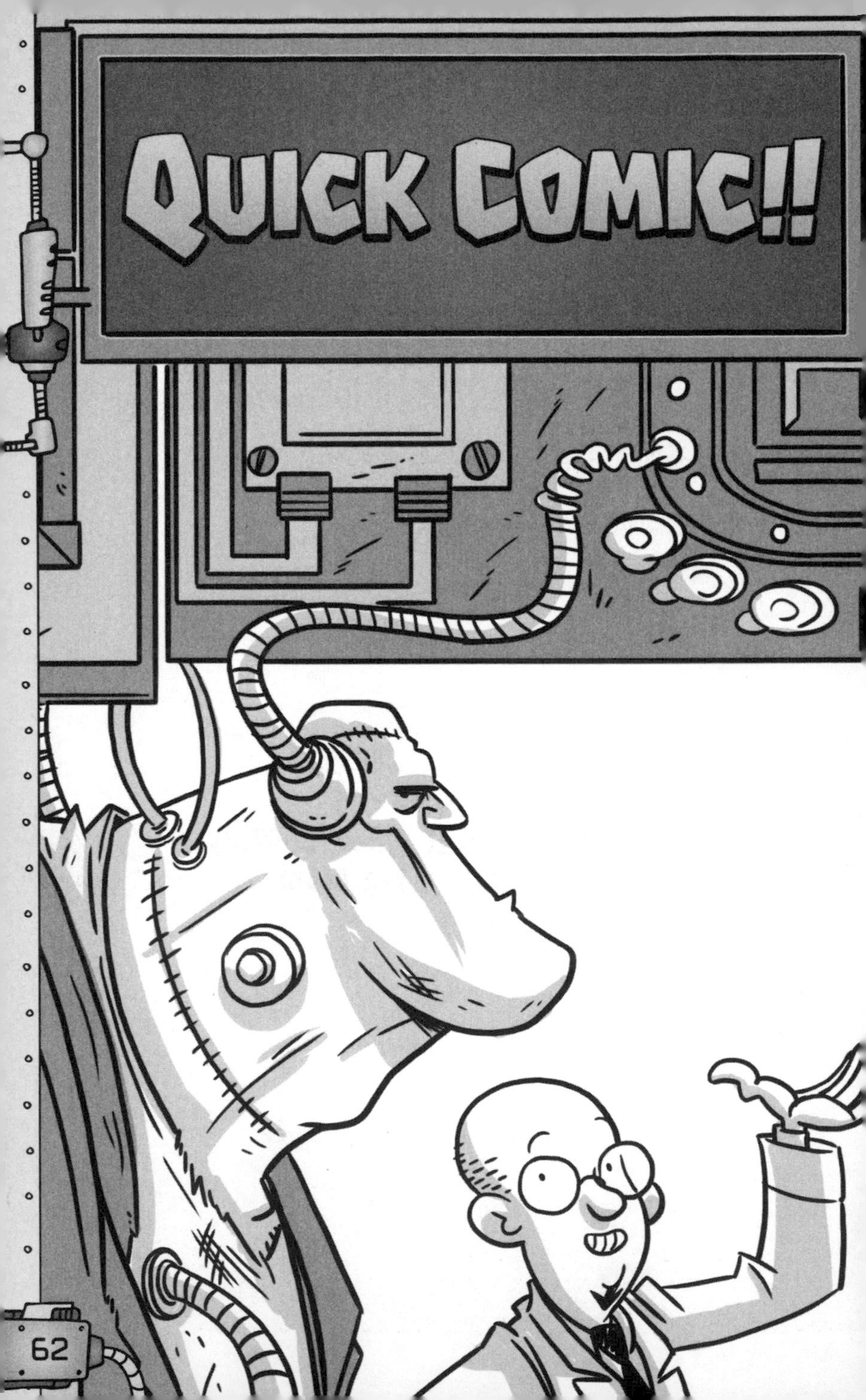
QUICK COMIC!!

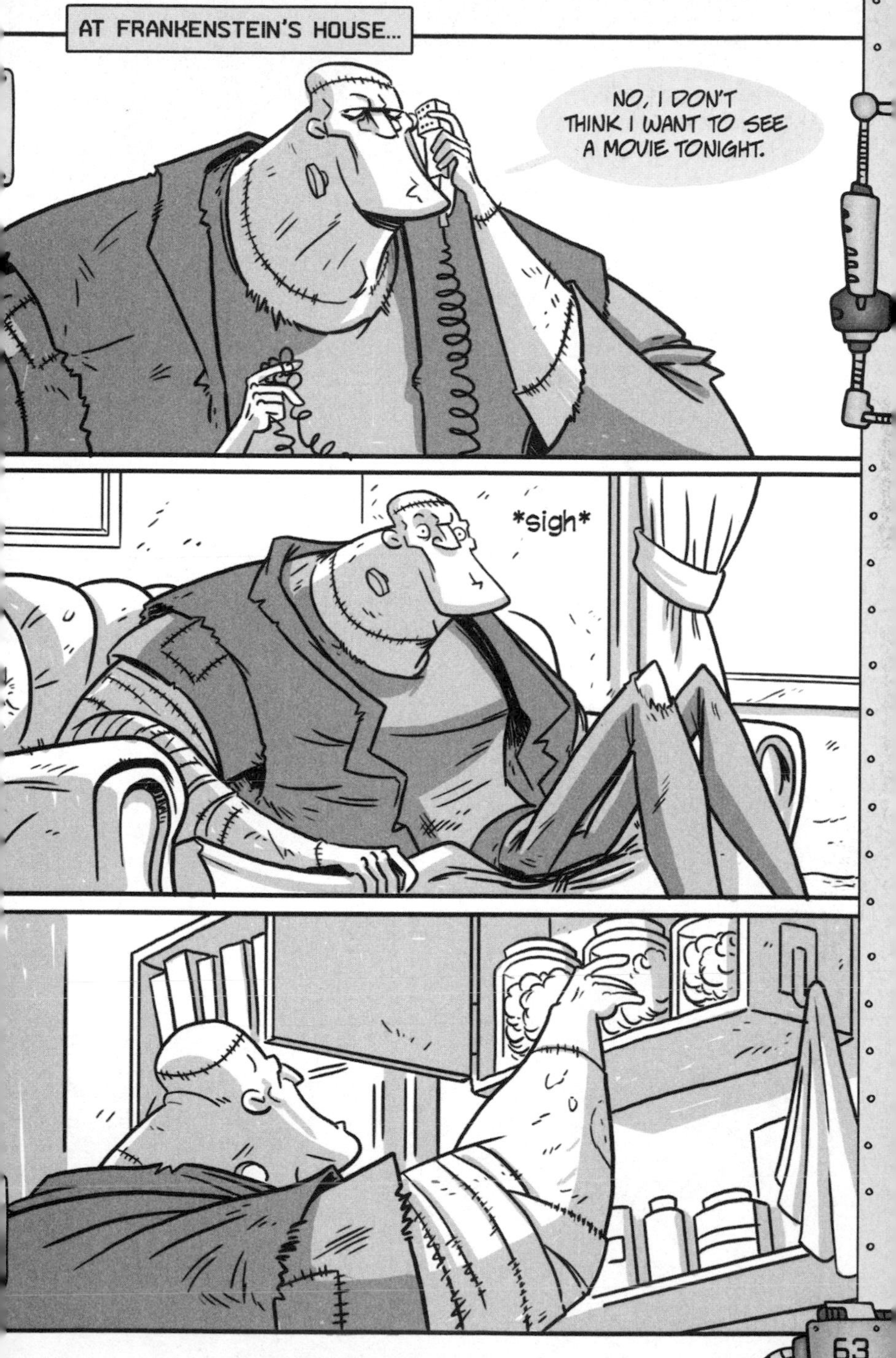
AT FRANKENSTEIN'S HOUSE...
NO, I DON'T THINK I WANT TO SEE A MOVIE TONIGHT.
sigh

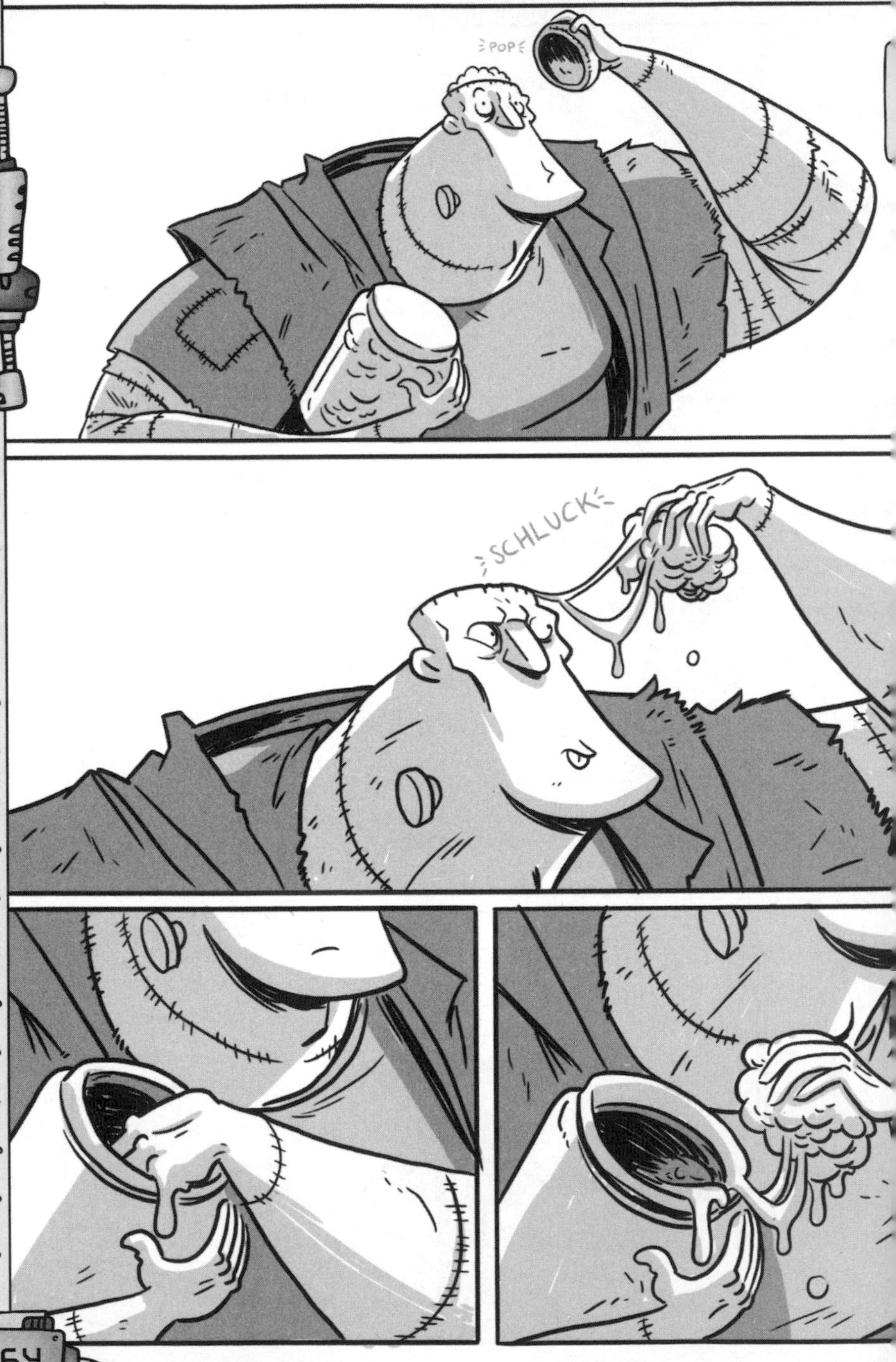
POP
SCHLUCK

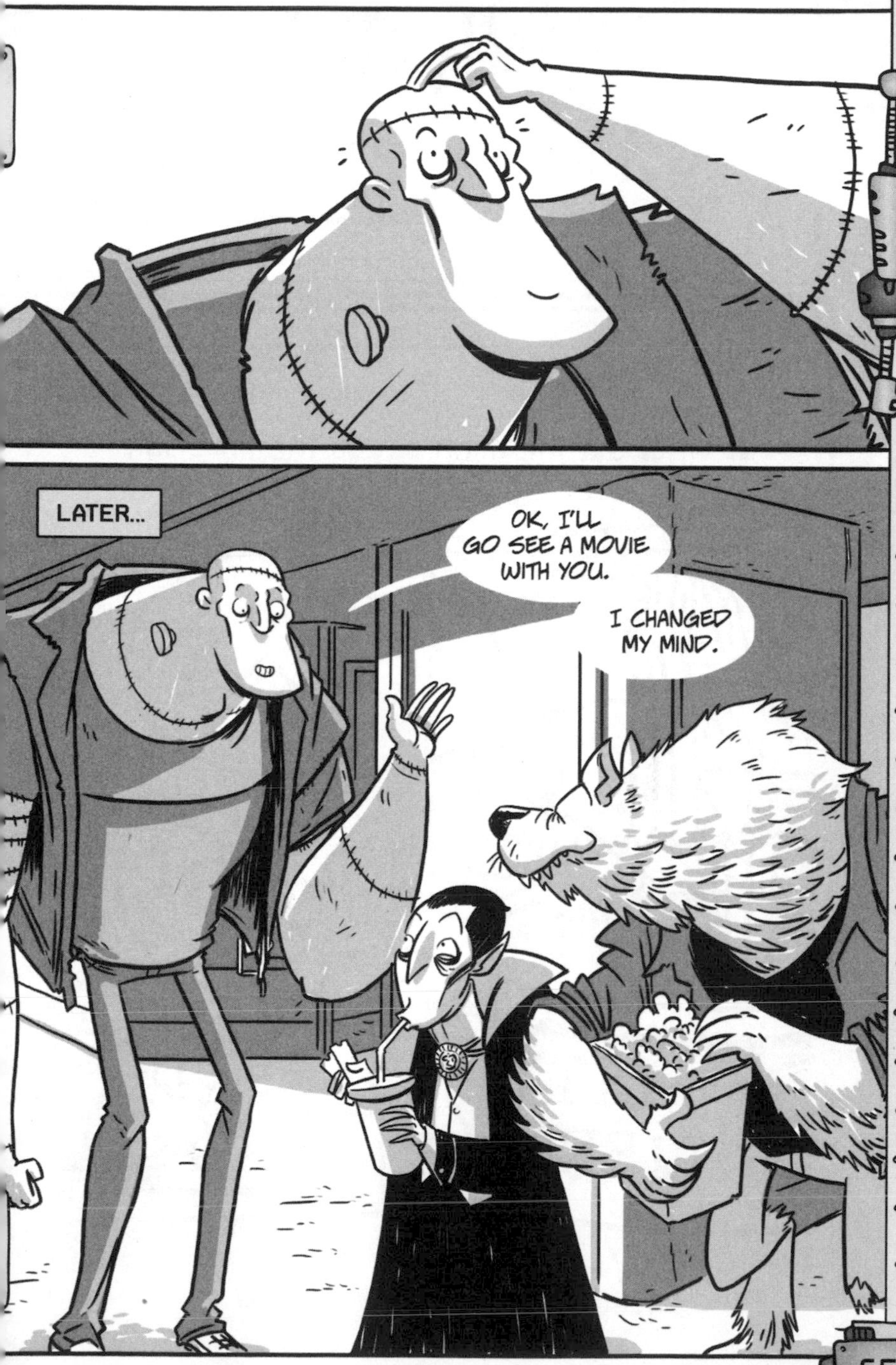
LATER...
OK, I'LL GO SEE A MOVIE WITH YOU.
I CHANGED MY MIND.

WHaT'd YOU SAY?

Q: What did the alien say to the librarian?

A: Take me to your reader!

Q: What did the alien say to the measuring cup?

A: Take me to your litre!

Q: What did the alien say to the gardener?

A: Take me to your weeder!

Q: What did the alien say to Dracula?

A: Take me to your bleeder!

LAFF-O-TRONIC

MONSTERS
Stand Up!

What did the audience say to Dracula during his stand-up routine?

"You suck!"

Why was the zombie so bad at telling jokes?

He fell apart on stage.

Why are zombies the best audience to perform for?

They always eat it up!

What did the stage manager yell to the mummy when he went overtime?

"Wrap it up!"

How did the werewolf do during his gig?
He was a howling success.

And what about Frankenstein?
He was electrifying!

What do zombies like to eat with tacos?
Refried beings.

Did you hear about the UFO that landed in a cow field?
It had close encounters of the herd kind.

What monster tree roams the forest?

Frankenpine.

Where can you find a house full of zombies?

On a dead end.

How do little ghosts keep cool during the summer?

They turn on the scare conditioner.

What has fangs and fleece as white as snow?

A lamb-pire!

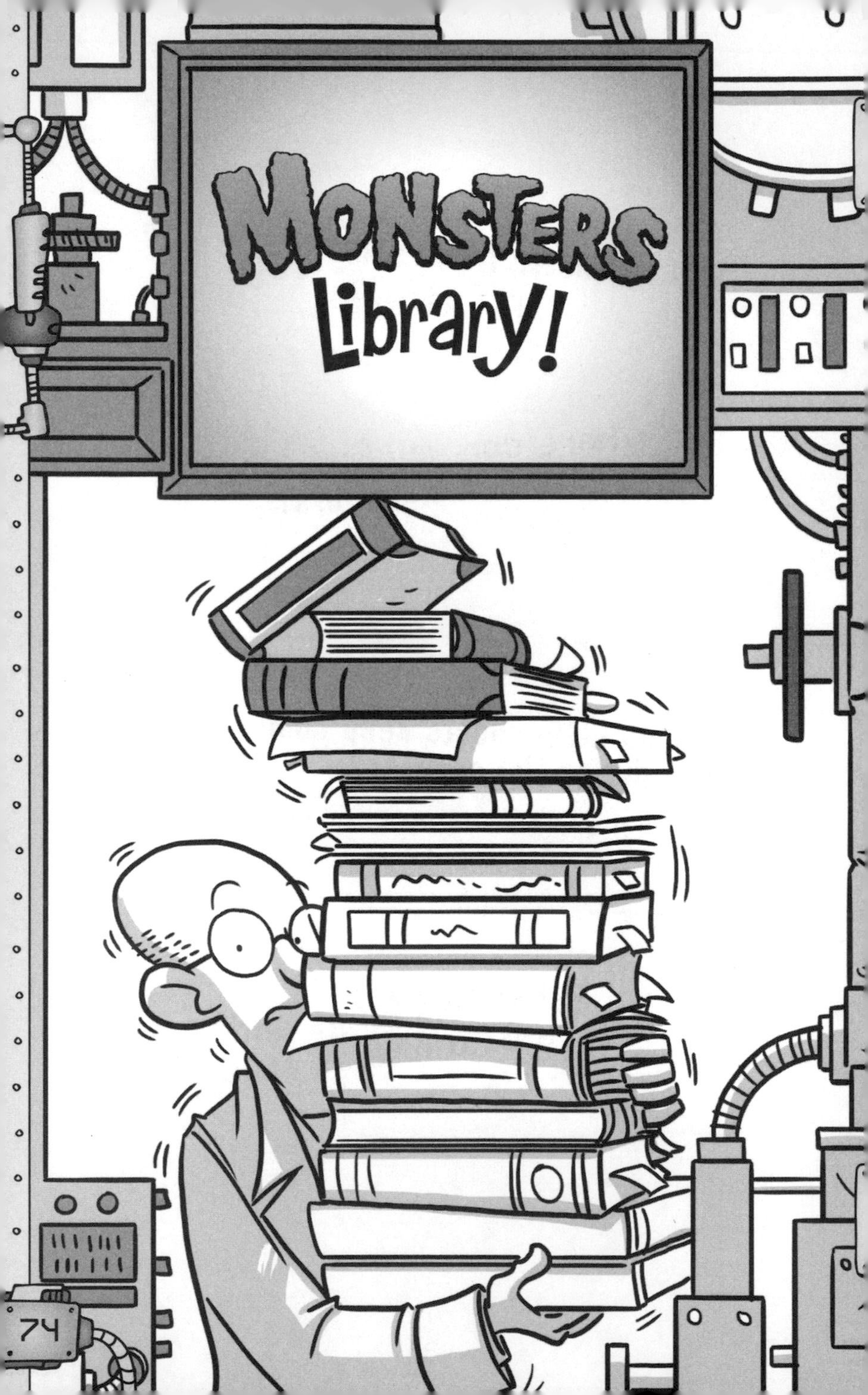
MONSTERS
Library!

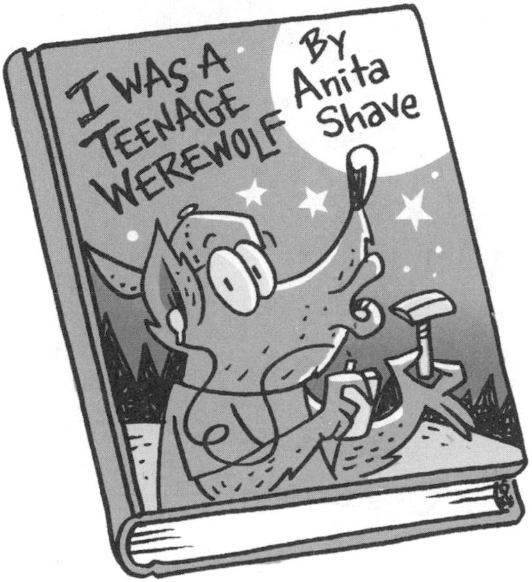
I WAS A TEENAGE WEREWOLF
By Anita Shave

It Screams At Midnight, by Waylon Moan

I Was A Teenage Werewolf, by Anita Shave

Attack of the Zombies, by Doug Moregraves

The Phantom Strangler, by Hans Archer Throte

Don't Go Out At Night!, by Freyda Thudark

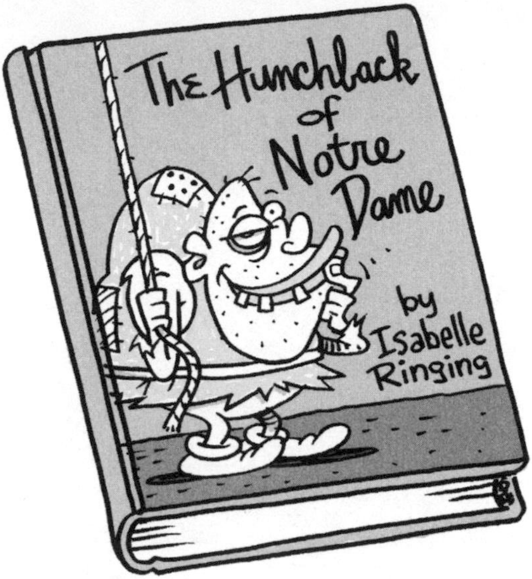
The Hunchback of Notre Dame
by Isabelle Ringing

The Fortune Teller, by Horace Cope

Chased by the Wolfman, by Claude S. Armoff

Invisible Ink, by M. T. Pages

The Hunchback of Notre Dame, by Isabelle Ringing

The Eyes of Medusa, by May Dove Stone

Aliens Have Landed! by Ross Well

A Zombie's Life, by Myra Maines

Making New Things, by N. Ventor

In the Laboratory, by Tess Tube

The World of the Unknown, by Misty Rees

Beware the Bride of Frankenstein, by Sheila Tack

Easy Recipes for the Busy Zombie, by Hugh Mann Bings

Into the Haunted House, by Hugo First

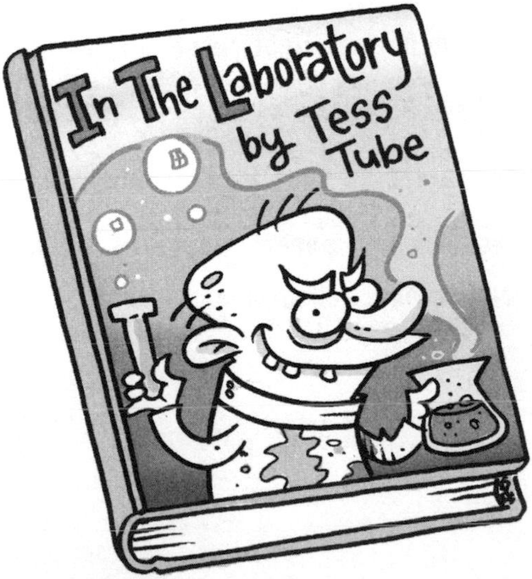
In The Laboratory
by Tess Tube

FLippin' OUT!

Dracula Suprise!

1. Grab the bottom-right corner of page 79.

2. Flip page 79 back and forth without letting go.

3. Keep an eye on page 81.

4. If you flip fast enough, pages 79 and 81 will look like one, animated picture!

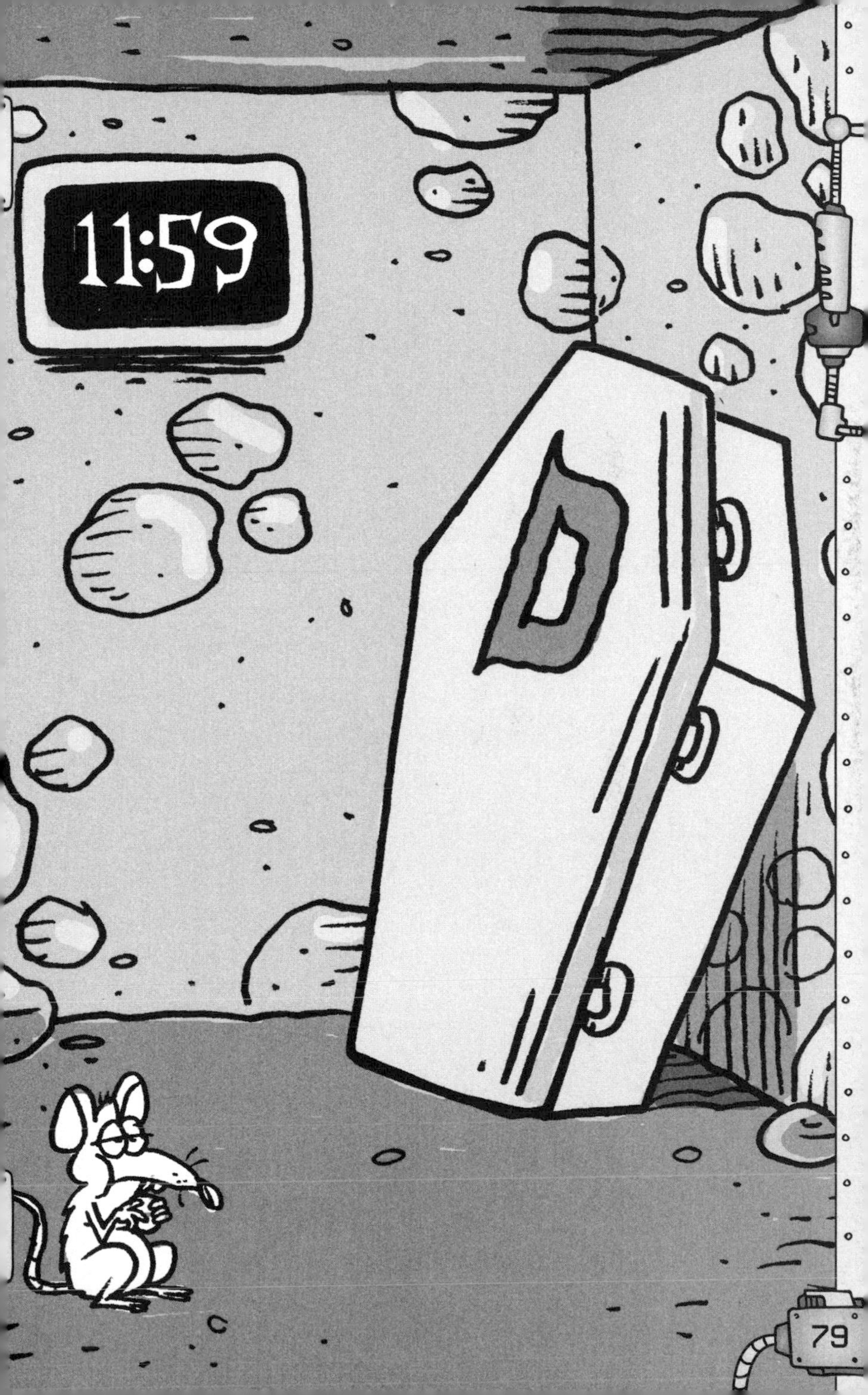
11:59
D

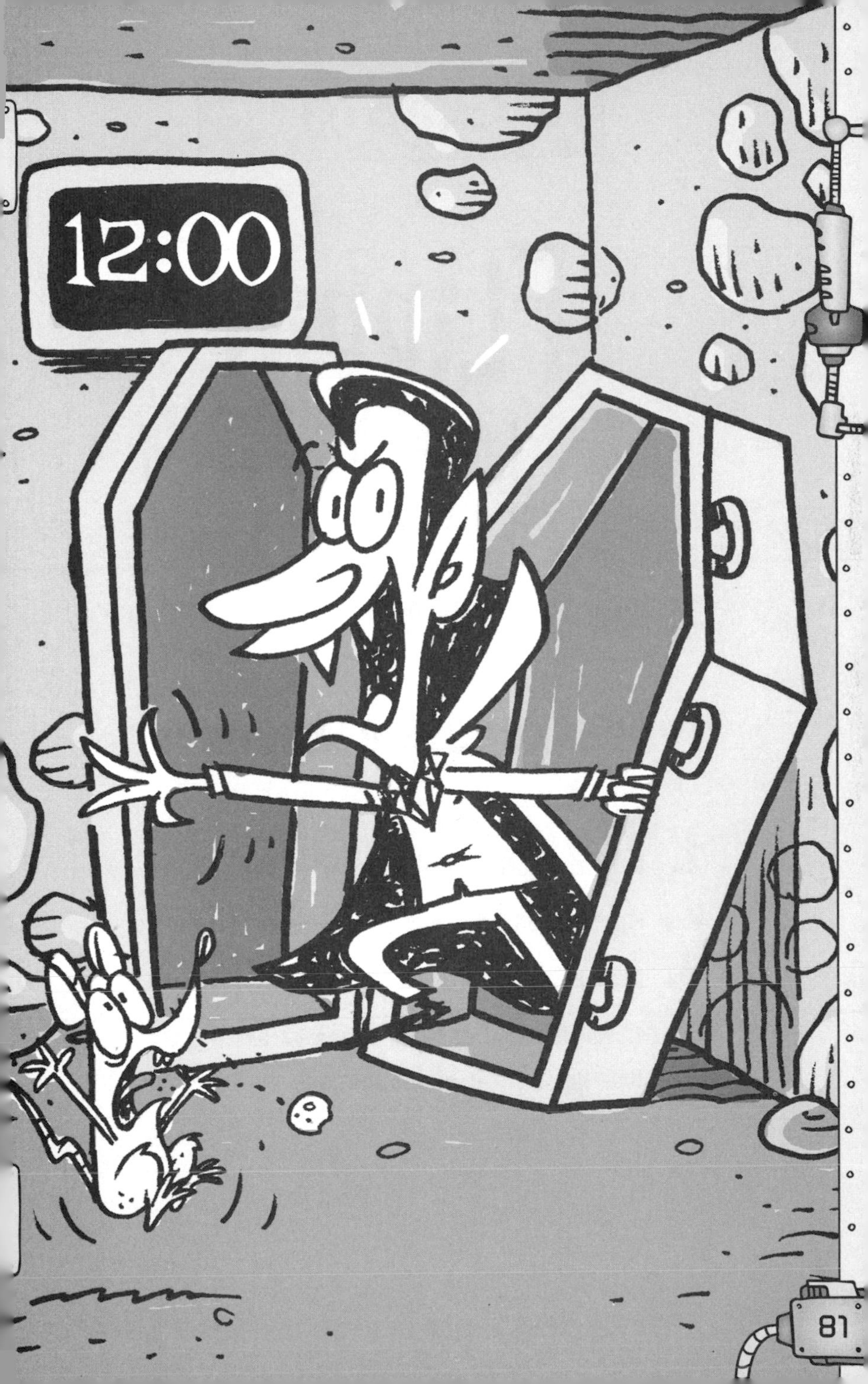
12:00

Flippin' OUT!

Frankenstein Shocker!

1. Grab the bottom-right corner of page 83.

2. Flip page 83 back and forth without letting go.

3. Keep an eye on page 85.

4. If you flip fast enough, pages 83 and 85 will look like one, animated picture!

82

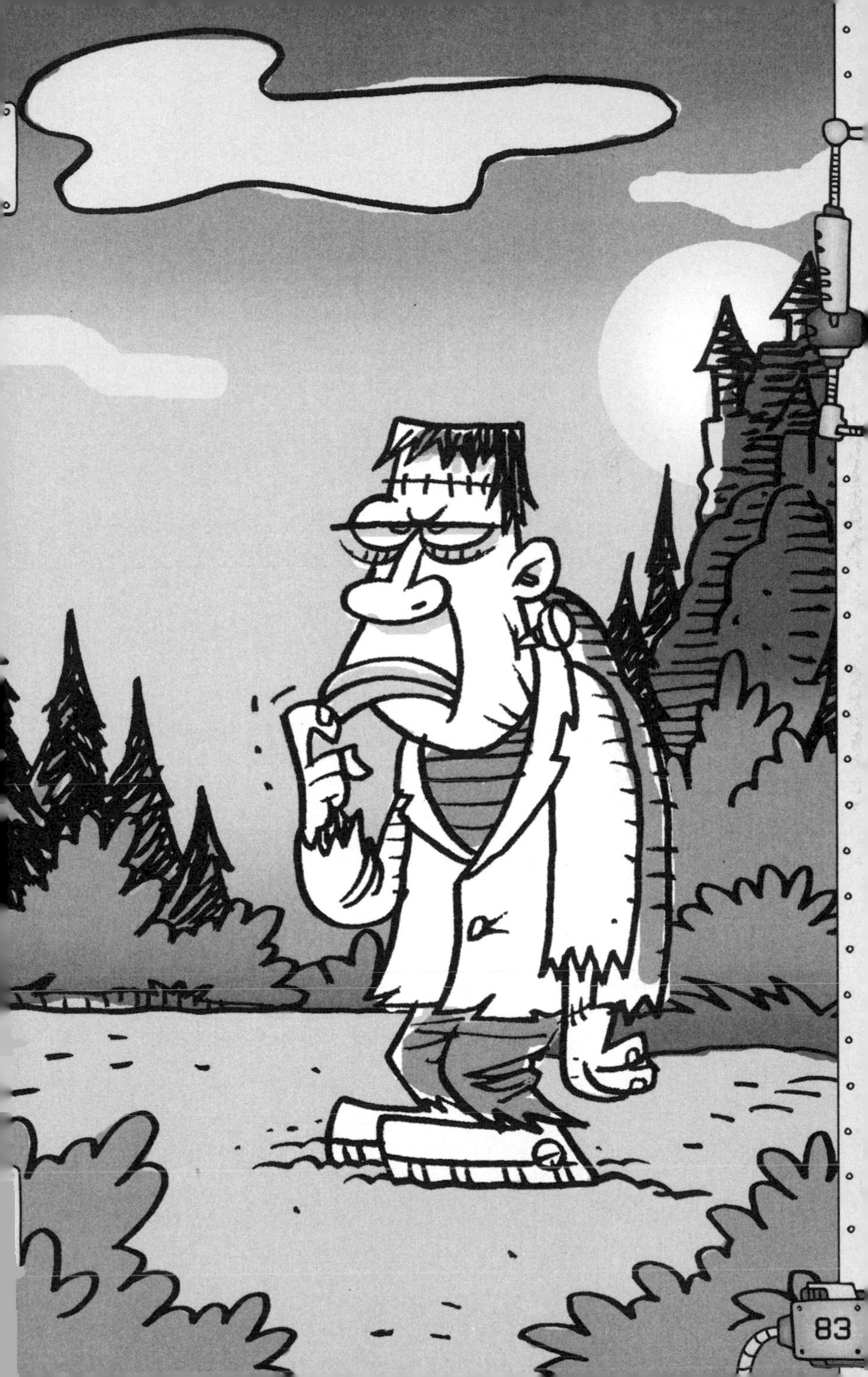

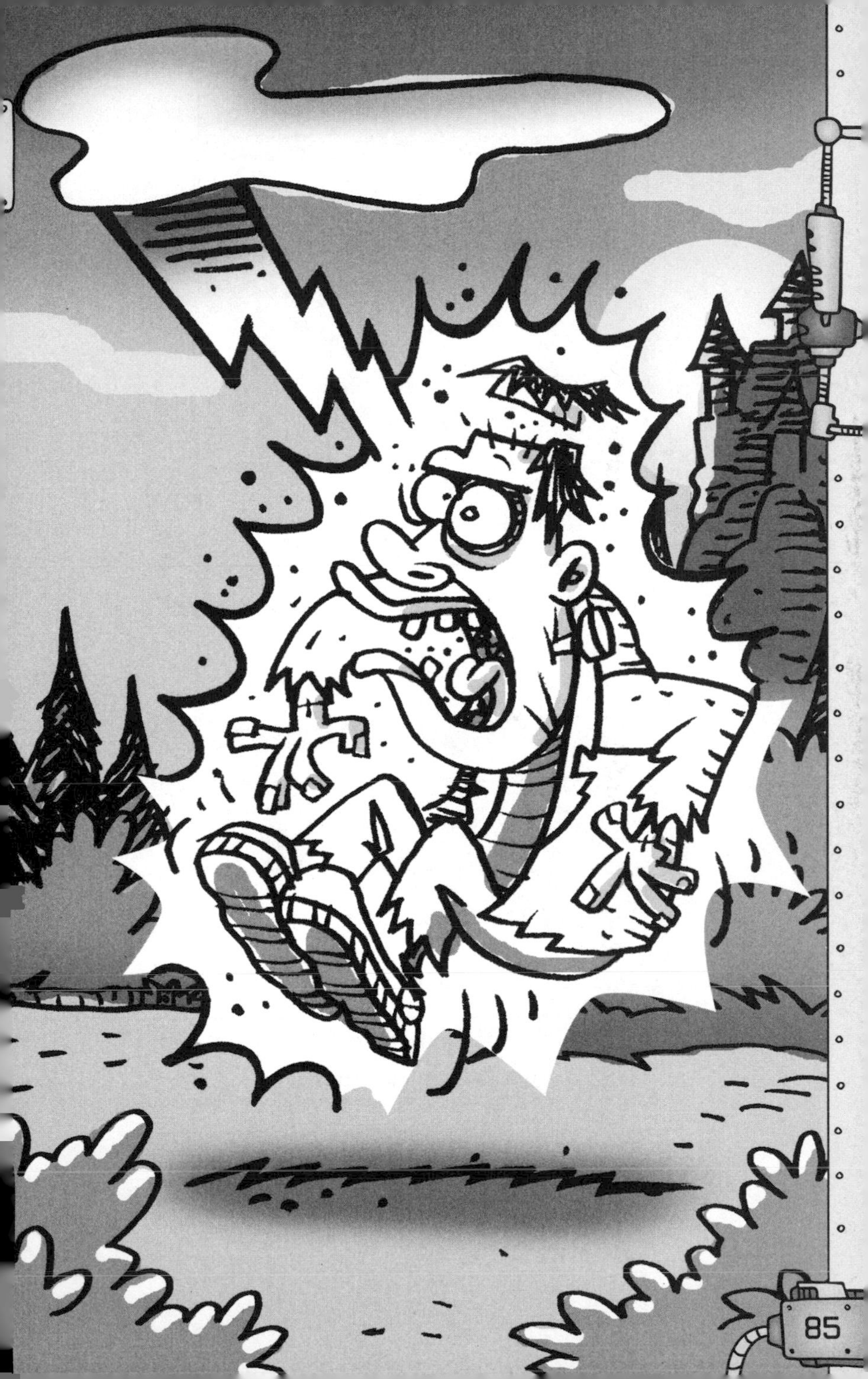

LAFF-O-TRONIC

FLippin' OUT!

Wolfman Changeup!

1. Grab the bottom-right corner of page 87.

2. Flip page 87 back and forth without letting go.

3. Keep an eye on page 89.

4. If you flip fast enough, pages 87 and 89 will look like one, animated picture!

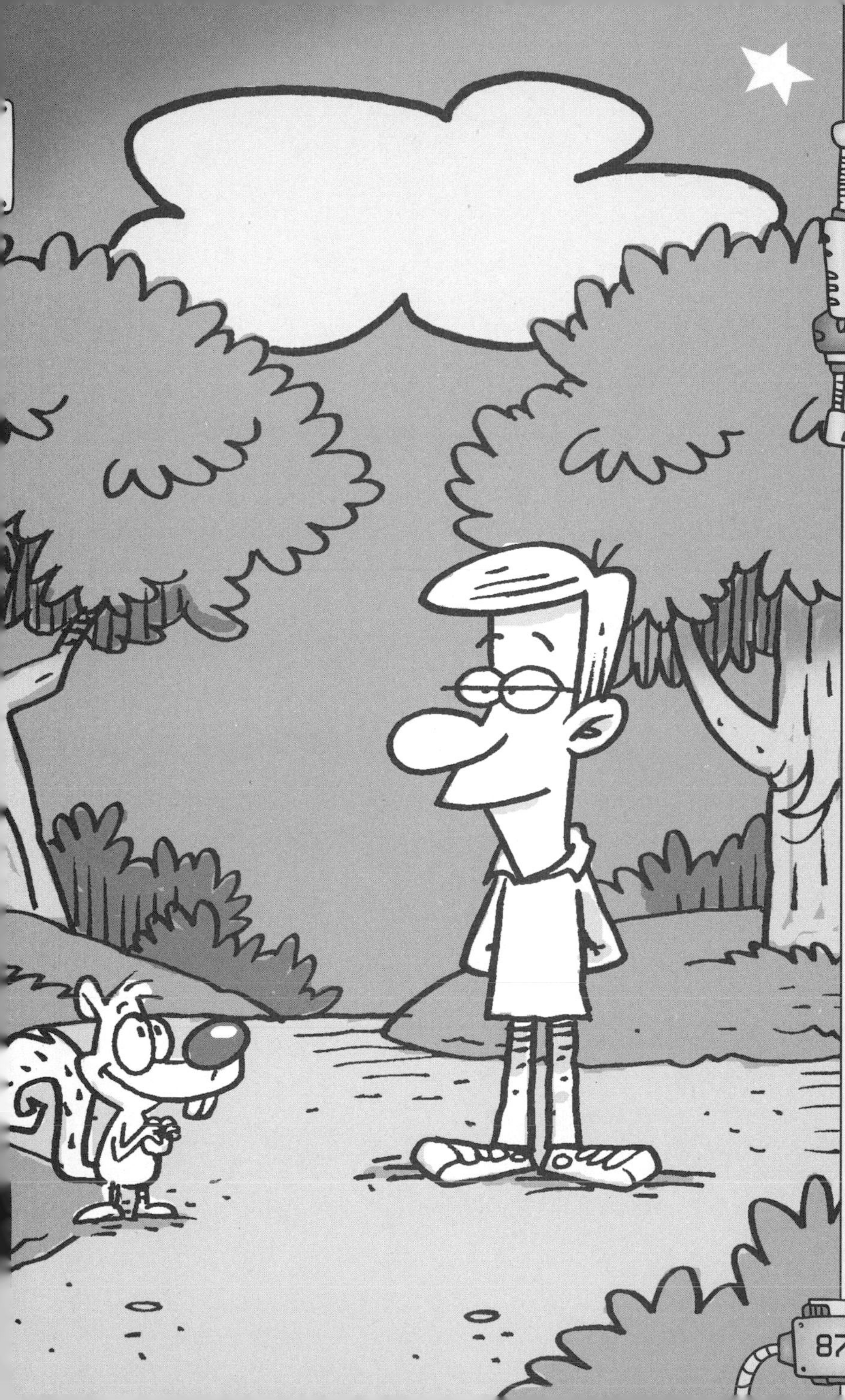

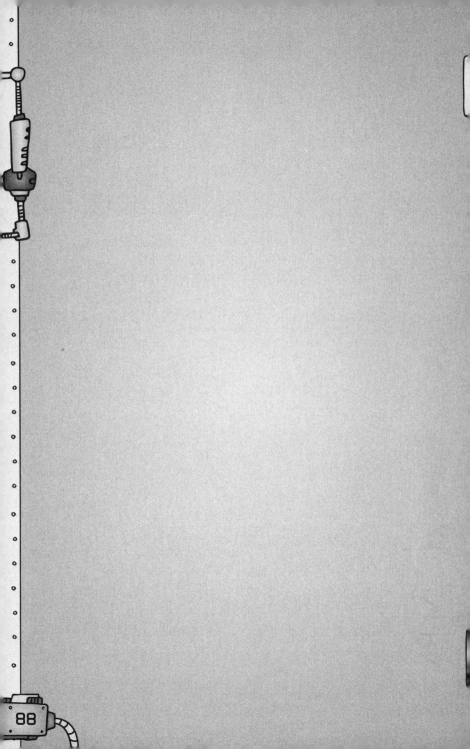

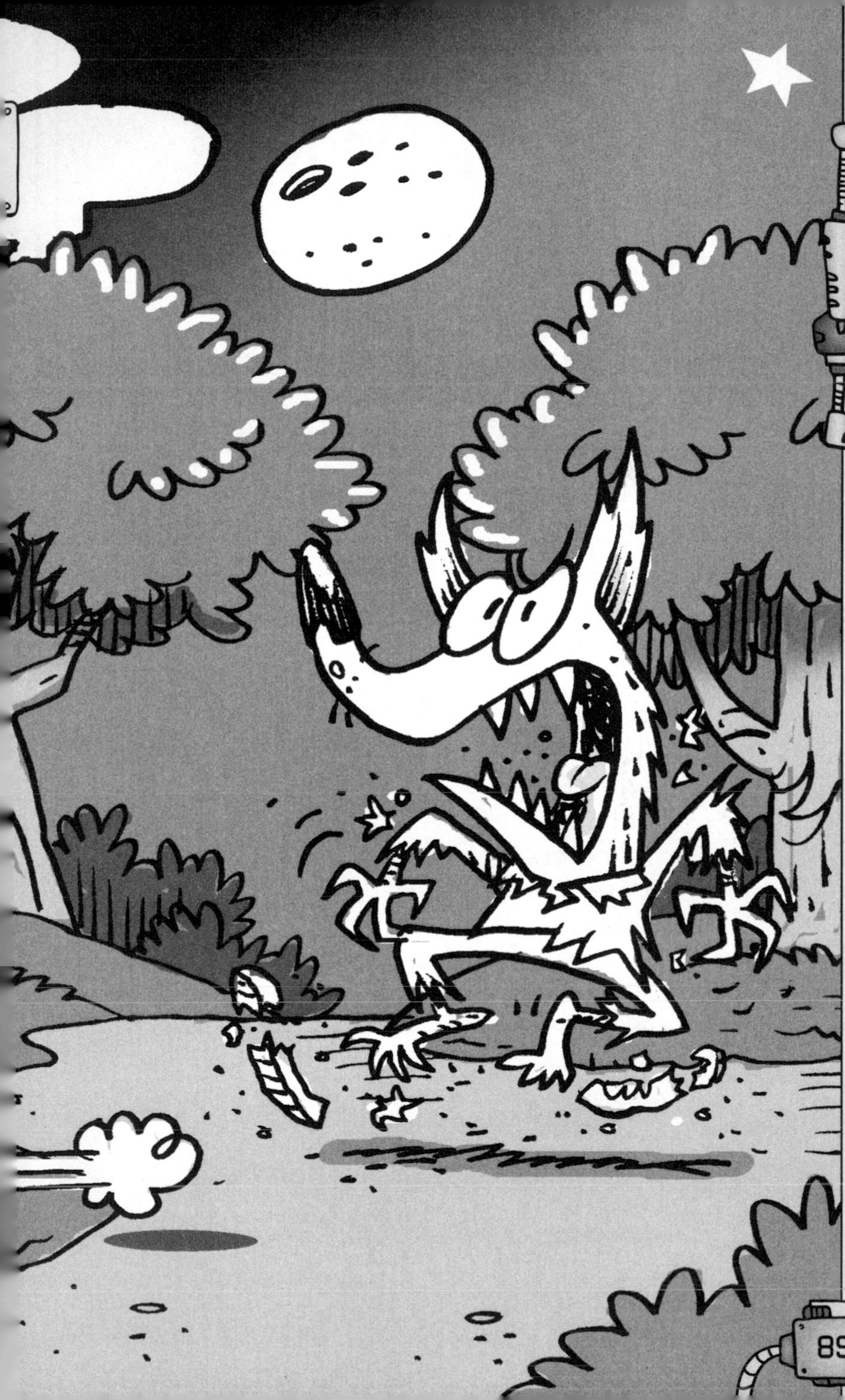

How to Draw FRANKENSTEIN!

(YOU'LL NEED A PENCIL, A PIECE OF PAPER, AND AN ERASER.)

1. USING YOUR PENCIL, DRAW A CIRCLE ON YOUR PAPER. THEN DRAW TWO LINES THROUGH THE CIRCLE, AS SHOWN AT RIGHT.

2. ADD AN EAR AND A LONG, SQUARE JAW TO YOUR MONSTER.

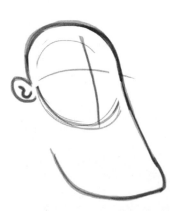

3. NEXT, DRAW TWO SMALL CIRCLES FOR EYEBALLS. MAKE SURE THE EYES LINE UP ON CENTER LINE. DON'T FORGET THE PUPILS!

4. THEN GIVE YOUR MONSTER A NOSE. WILL HE HAVE A GIANT SCHNOZ OR A BITTY BEAK? YOU DECIDE!

5. ERASE THE TWO LINES FROM STEP #1. THEN ADD DETAILS TO YOUR MONSTER. GIVE HIM STITCHES, BOLTS, AND A FUNNY SMILE!

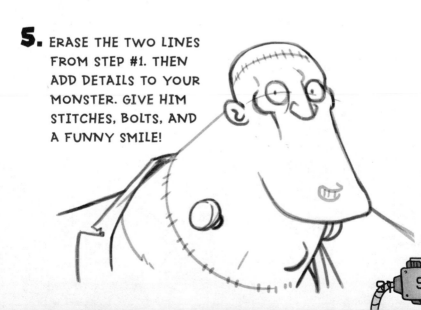

AUTHOR

MICHAEL DAHL

HAS WRITTEN MORE THAN 200 BOOKS FOR YOUNG READERS. HE IS THE AUTHOR OF THE SUPER-FUNNY JOKE BOOKS SERIES, ***THE EVERYTHING KIDS' JOKE BOOKS,*** THE SCINTILLATING ***DUCK GOES POTTY,*** AND TWO HUMOROUS MYSTERY SERIES: FINNEGAN ZWAKE (A "WISECRACKING RIOT" ACCORDING TO THE ***CHICAGO TRIBUNE***) AND HOCUS POCUS HOTEL. HE TOURED THE COUNTRY WITH AN IMPROV TROUPE, AND BEGAN HIS AUSPICIOUS COMIC CAREER IN 5TH GRADE WHEN HIS STAND-UP ROUTINE MADE HIS MUSIC TEACHER LAUGH SO HARD SHE FELL OFF HER CHAIR. SHE IS NOT AVAILABLE FOR COMMENT.

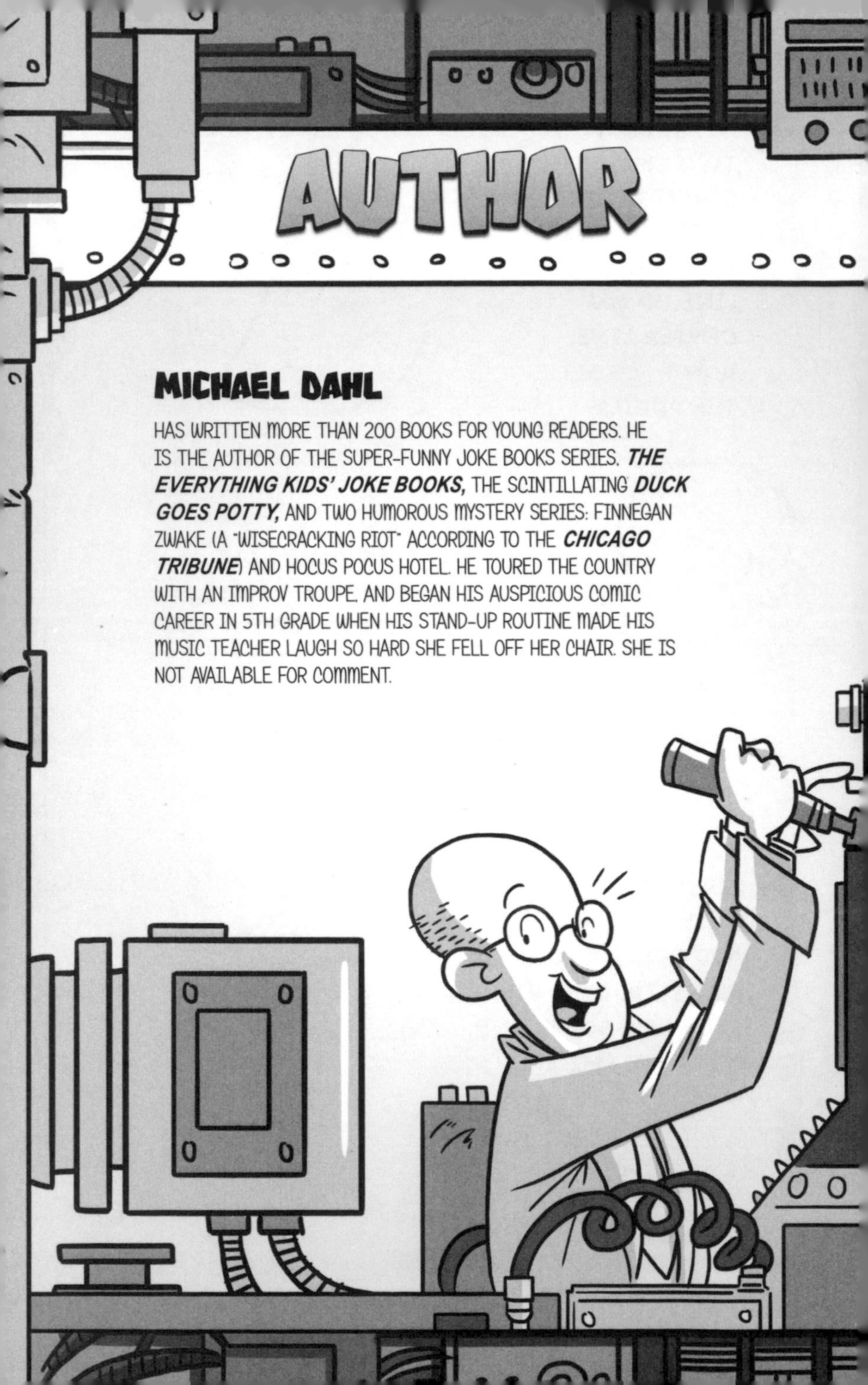

ILLUSTRATORS

DOUGLAS HOLGATE

IS A FREELANCE ILLUSTRATOR, COMIC BOOK ARTIST, AND CARTOONIST BASED IN MELBOURNE, AUSTRALIA. HIS WORK HAS BEEN PUBLISHED ALL AROUND THE WORLD BY RANDOM HOUSE, SIMON AND SCHUSTER, THE NEW YORKER MAGAZINE, MAD MAGAZINE, IMAGE COMICS, AND MANY OTHERS. HIS WORKS FOR CHILDREN INCLUDE THE ZINC ALLOY AND BIKE RIDER SERIES (CAPSTONE), SUPER CHICKEN NUGGET BOY (HYPERION), AND A NEW SERIES OF POPULAR SCIENCE BOOKS BY DR. KARL KRUSZELNICKI (PAN MACMILLAN). DOUGLAS HAS SPORTED A POWERFUL, MANLY BEARD SINCE AGE 12 (PROBABLY NOT TRUE) AND IS ALSO A PRETTY RAD DUDE (PROBABLY TRUE).

DARYLL COLLINS

IS A FREELANCE CARTOONIST WHOSE WORK HAS APPEARED IN BOOKS, MAGAZINES, COMIC STRIPS, ADVERTISING, GREETING CARDS, PRODUCT PACKAGING AND CHARACTER DESIGN. HE ENJOYS MUSIC, MOVIES, BASEBALL, FOOTBALL, COFFEE, PIZZA, PETS, AND OF COURSE... CARTOONS!

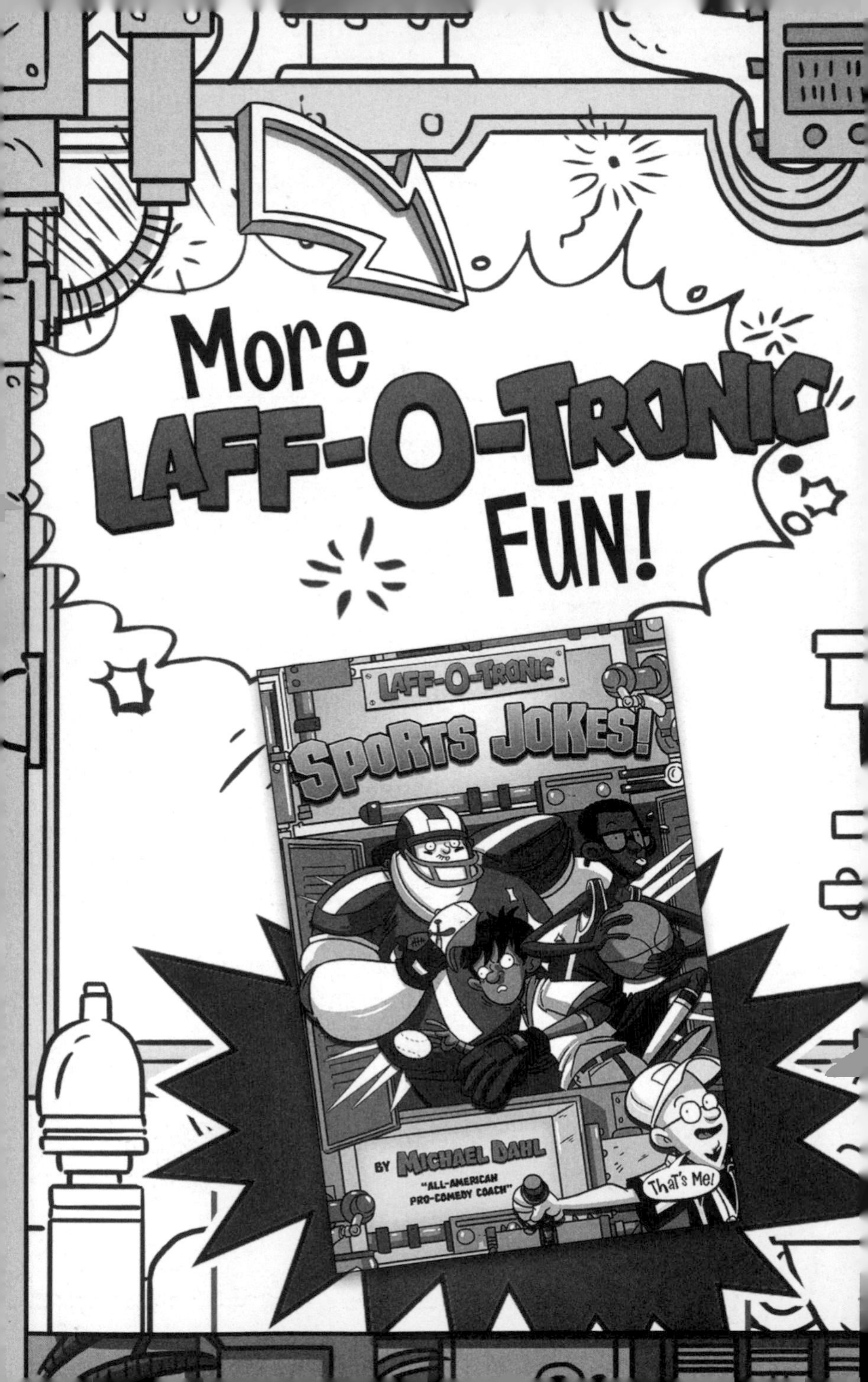
More
LAFF-O-TRONIC
FUN!
LAFF-O-TRONIC
SPORTS JOKES!
BY MICHAEL DAHL
"ALL-AMERICAN PRO-COMEDY COACH"
That's Me!

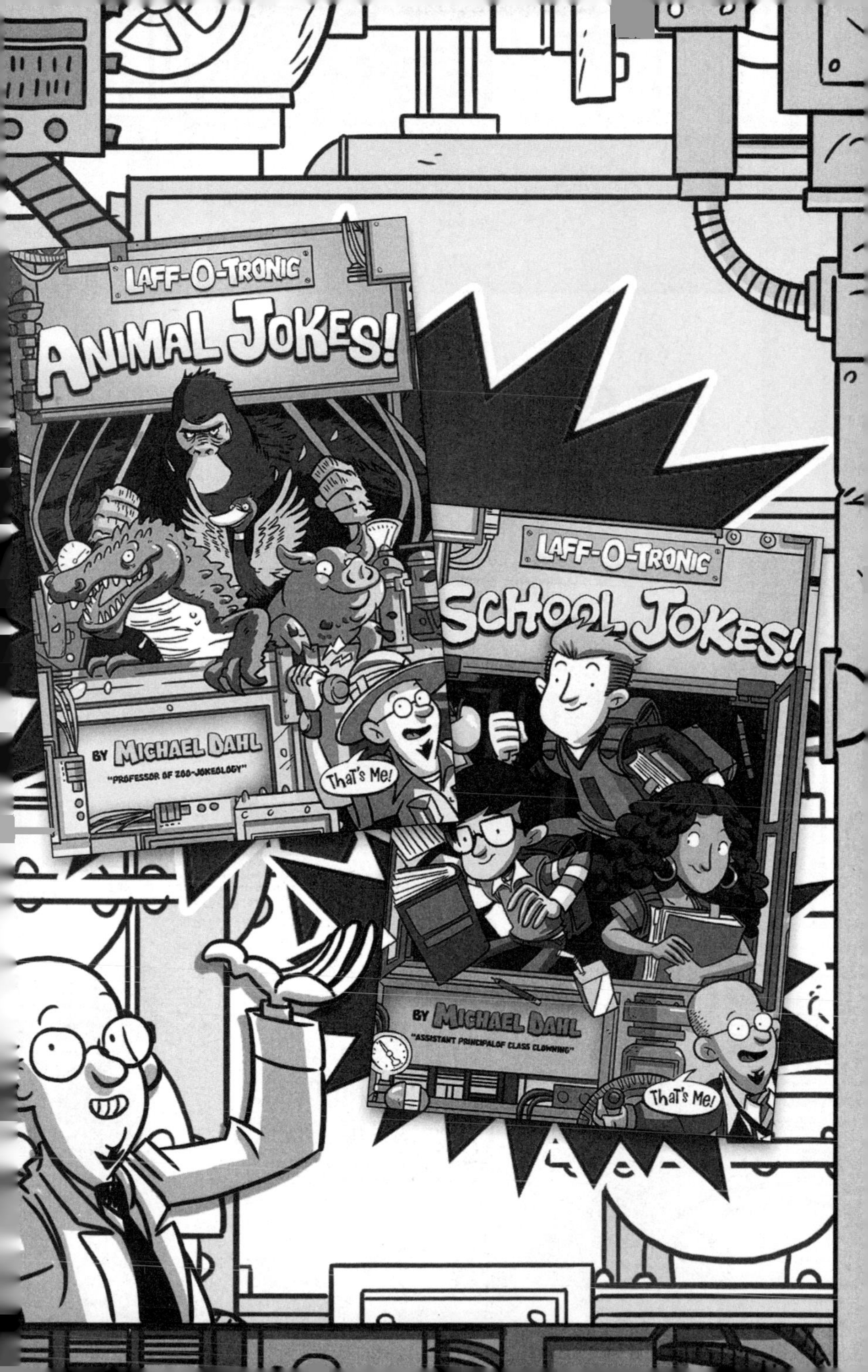
LAFF-O-TRONIC
ANIMAL JOKES!
BY MICHAEL DAHL
"PROFESSOR OF ZOO-JOKEOLOGY"
That's Me!
LAFF-O-TRONIC
SCHOOL JOKES!
BY MICHAEL DAHL
"ASSISTANT PRINCIPALOF CLASS CLOWNING"
That's Me!

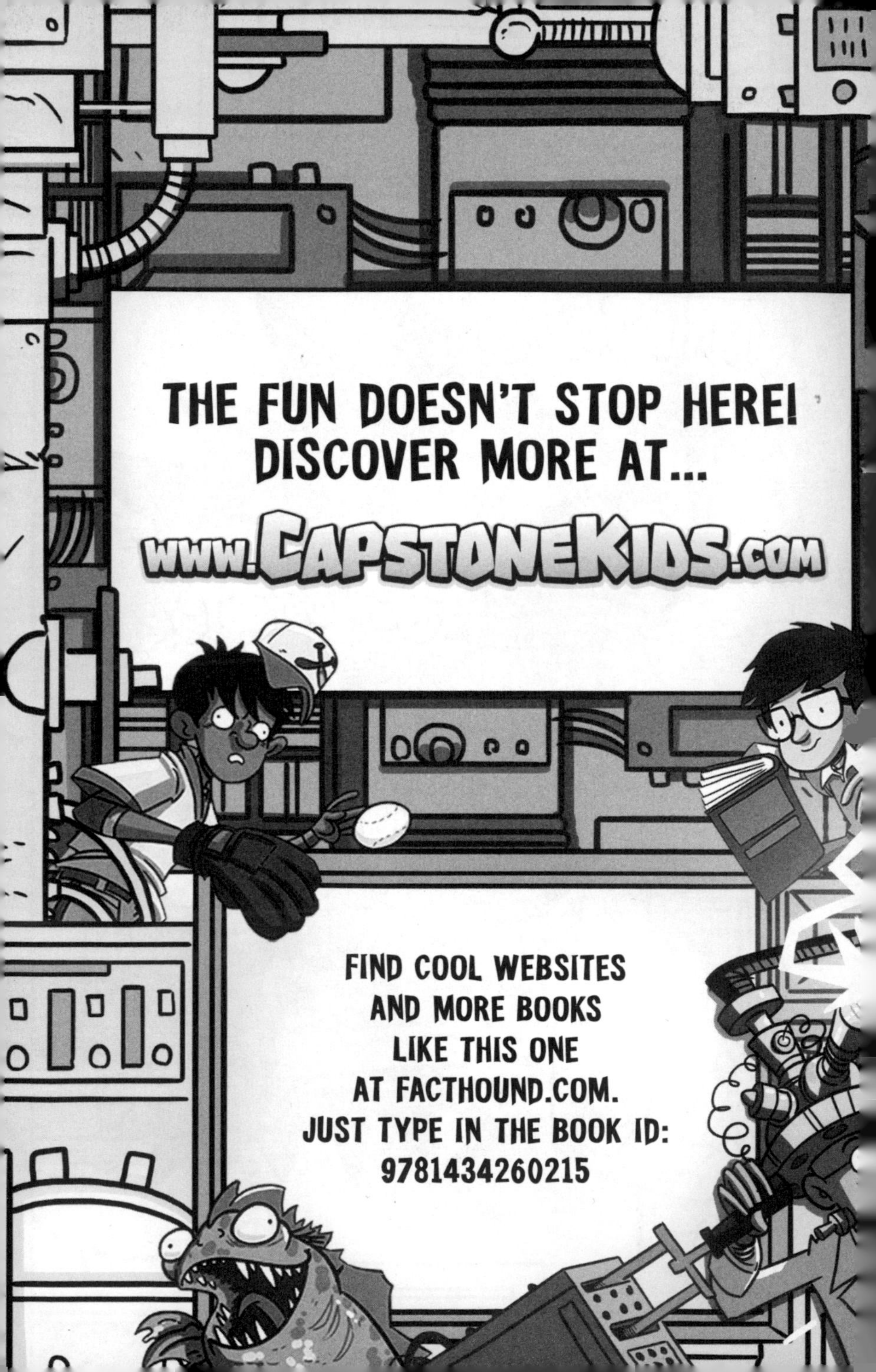
THE FUN DOESN'T STOP HERE!
DISCOVER MORE AT...
www.CAPSTONEKIDS.com
FIND COOL WEBSITES
AND MORE BOOKS
LIKE THIS ONE
AT FACTHOUND.COM.
JUST TYPE IN THE BOOK ID:
9781434260215